LEADER LION

LEADER LION

PROTECTION, INC.
5

ZOE CHANT

ROM
Chant

THE PROTECTION, INC. SERIES

Bodyguard Bear
Defender Dragon
Protector Panther
Warrior Wolf
Leader Lion
Soldier Snow Leopard
Top Gun Tiger (forthcoming)

All the books in the series are standalone romances. Each focuses on a new couple, with no cliffhangers. They can be read in any order. But characters from previous books reappear in later ones, so reading in order is recommended for maximum enjoyment.

TABLE OF CONTENTS

Chapter One	1
Chapter Two	7
Chapter Three	17
Chapter Four	25
Chapter Five	31
Chapter Six	41
Chapter Seven	59
Chapter Eight	67
Chapter Nine	75
Chapter Ten	87
Chapter Eleven	93
Chapter Twelve	99
Chapter Thirteen	111
Chapter Fourteen	121
Chapter Fifteen	137
Chapter Sixteen	141
Chapter Seventeen	147
Chapter Eighteen	151
Chapter Nineteen	161
Epilogue	173
A note from Zoe Chant	179
Zoe Chant Complete Book List	181
Soldier Snow Leopard Sneak Preview	187

CHAPTER ONE

Rafa

Rafa Flores was done with one-night stands.

But he was never, ever going to admit it. Ever. Especially not to his annoyingly happy mated friends who kept telling him to give up the flings and go find his own mate. As if it was that easy!

So Rafa plastered on a smug grin for his teammate Nick, who had just elbowed him in the ribs and said, "Hey, Rafa, your shirt's unbuttoned. Did your stripper-of-the-night grab you by it on your way out the door?"

"One: model, not stripper," Rafa replied. "And two: there were two of them. Blonde… gorgeous… *twins.* Identical."

The entire team had gathered at Protection, Inc. after their boss Hal had called them in, along with the mates of everyone who had mates, so Hal and *his* mate could tell them some good news in person. He'd greeted them all in the lobby as he stood with his arm around Ellie, his sweet and brave paramedic mate.

Rafa had a pretty good idea of what the news would be, and from the excited way everyone had been watching Hal and Ellie, they all did too. But once Rafa had claimed that he'd left twin models in his bed, everybody turned to stare at him.

Hal and Ellie only glanced at him for a second before they went back to gazing lovingly at each other, with curvy little Ellie nestled against Hal's huge side. They were clearly too wrapped up in each other and their big news to care if Rafa had just had sex with every single contestant on *America's Top Model.* Simultaneously.

Nick looked reluctantly impressed. Then he folded his arms across his chest, making the sleeves of his black leather jacket ride up and expose more of his werewolf gang tattoos, and muttered, "Whatever, Rafa. Hope you left them identical fucking mugs of coffee."

Nick's dragon shifter mate, Raluca, raised her elegant silver eyebrows at Rafa in mild revulsion. She'd once been a princess, and Rafa could see her royal training in both how tacky she clearly found his announcement and how much better she was than Nick at dropping her initial expression and replacing it with one of cool unconcern.

Lucas, who had also once been royalty, and his free-spirited mate Journey gave Rafa a pair of "what the hell" glances, then returned their gazes to Hal and Ellie, whose upcoming news they clearly found much more interesting than anything Rafa could possibly get up to in bed.

Catalina, the newest member of the bodyguard team, grinned at Rafa. "Wow, twins. What an adventure! I hope you all had fun."

Rafa made sure he sounded blissfully satisfied when he replied, "It was unforgettable for all three of us."

But his teammates Fiona and Shane kept right on eyeing him with similar— no, *identical*— looks of suspicion in her clear green eyes and his icy blue ones. Obviously neither of them believed a word he'd said. But they wouldn't contradict him; they had enough secrets of their own to know how to keep one.

His teammate Destiny's shoulders shook with barely-suppressed laughter. As he watched, she ducked her head, sending her box braids flying around her face, and actually stuffed her knuckles against her mouth to stifle her snickers. She obviously didn't buy his story either. Rafa was sure the only reason she wasn't jumping all over him was because she didn't want to step on Hal and Ellie's moment, but intended to tease the hell out of him later.

In fact, Fiona, Destiny, and Shane were right. There were no models, twins or otherwise. The depressing truth was that Rafa had leaned over his cold and empty bed to take Hal's call, guessed what the news would be, and had been so torn between happiness for his best friend and gloom at the thought that he'd never be able to make the same announcement himself that he'd forgotten to button his shirt.

Rafa hurriedly zipped his jacket over it.

Hal cleared his throat. In his rumbling voice, he began, "Guys…"

"And ladies," Raluca put in.

"And ladies," Hal echoed with a grin. "Ellie, take it away."

If Rafa hadn't guessed already, he would have then. Ellie had the proverbial glow all over her. Her soft curves were plumper than usual, her cheeks were pinker, her blue-green eyes were brighter, and even her sandy blonde hair seemed more curly, as if it had been infused with extra life.

"We're pregnant!" Ellie announced. Then her cheeks went even pinker. "I mean, *I'm* pregnant. *We're* going to have a baby!"

Hal's deep tones cut through the chorus of congratulations that instantly arose. "Two babies. Ellie's having twins!"

That part did surprise Rafa. "Congratulations! That's fantastic!"

"Yeah, that's great!" Destiny said to Ellie and Hal. Then she jabbed Rafa in the ribs, hitting the exact same spot Nick had already smacked. "Twins. What a coincidence."

Rafa stifled a groan. Of all the times for him to invent imaginary twins! Now his teammates would never let him hear the end of it.

"They run in the family," Ellie said. A brief shadow flickered across her face, dimming her happy smile. She was a twin herself, with a brother who was a Recon Marine. "Don't be afraid to mention Ethan, guys. I know you're all thinking about him. He'd be here if he could. But he's on another hush-hush mission who knows where, the sort where you can't get phone calls. He'll have to get the good news when he comes back."

Rafa felt an odd mixture of sympathy and nostalgia at her words. He and Hal had once been on the same Navy SEAL team, so he knew all about no-call secret missions and missing important family news for months.

"I hope he'll be home in time for Christmas," Rafa said, his voice pitched to only be heard by Ellie and Hal.

"Thanks," said Hal.

Ellie gave Rafa a wistful smile, clearly appreciating his words but not thinking them very likely. "Yeah. Me too."

Another flood of congratulations and questions rose up.

"Boys or girls or one of each?" Catalina asked.

"Fraternal or… ah… identical?" Raluca inquired, then shot Rafa a quick but cutting glare to make it clear that she did not appreciate him making her embarrassed to ask the obvious question.

"Or do you know?" Shane didn't seem the slightest bit perturbed by the twin issue, to Rafa's relief. But that had nothing to do with Rafa; Shane was imperturbable.

"We're letting it be a surprise," Hal replied. "On all counts."

"Have you already selected possible names?" Lucas asked.

"When's the baby shower?" Journey called out.

Catalina stifled her, whispering, "We'll throw it."

"Fucking awesome, man," Nick said, his green eyes glittering with excitement. "Two at once—that's a fucking great start on a pack. I mean family. Twins! Fuck yeah!"

For the millionth time, Rafa thought, *How the hell did* Nick *find his mate when I'm still alone?*

It wasn't that he didn't like Nick. He loved Nick like a brother, the same as he loved all his teammates. In fact, he loved Nick *just* like a brother—the sort of little brother who annoyed the living daylights out of you and needed to be thoroughly teased on a regular basis to keep him in line.

But seriously, *Nick?* The hot-tempered ex-gangster who couldn't open his mouth without dropping eleven f-bombs? How had he found an elegant, intelligent, courageous, *former princess* dragon shifter mate when Rafa, who everyone said was quite a catch, had been left out in the cold?

Rafa didn't begrudge Nick his happiness. All the same, to borrow Nick's own words, life could be fucking unfair.

Rafa shook his head, sending his mane of black hair flying around his face and tossing the thought away with it. He was fine with being single. He had complete freedom. No howling babies to give him sleepless nights. If he wanted sex, all he had to do was stroll into a bar, find a pretty woman sitting alone, and smile at her.

Who needed mates, anyway?

We do, rumbled his lion. *And we're done with one-night stands. Remember?*

Stop reminding me, he replied silently.

His lion was the worst at jarring him out of fantasies that his life really was as perfect as other people thought it was. Now it was impossible for him to forget that babysitting Ellie and Hal's twins would be the closest he'd ever get to having children.

Just like watching his teammates find their mates was the closest he'd ever get to finding his own.

CHAPTER TWO

Grace

Grace Chang was done with handsome men.

And not just handsome men. She was also done with sexy men, suave men, charming men, men with easy smiles, men with funny banter, and men with suspiciously polished manners. Any extra-hot man who tried extra-hard to make a good impression had to have something wrong with him that he was trying to cover up. He'd turn out to be a cheater or a jerk or a criminal. Or, like Dean, her handsome, sexy, suave, charming, smiling, bantering, well-mannered ex-boyfriend, all of the above.

She settled back into her seat in the front row of the theatre, adjusted her clipboard and laptop, and scowled at the gorgeous actors singing their hearts out onstage. The lights were out in the audience but lit the chorus and the set brilliantly, shining right into the actors' eyes. Grace could glare all she wanted, safe in the knowledge that no one onstage could see. And since she was the stage manager and controlled the lights, along with the sound and the set changes, she'd always have advance warning to adjust her expression.

Actors! Handsome. Charming. Sexy. And bad, bad, *bad* news.

Grace had been fooled once. But it would never happen again. Oh, she wasn't swearing off all men forever. Just the ones who were clearly too good to be true. The next man she dated might not set her body on fire, but he'd also never cheat on her with sixteen strippers while committing credit card fraud in his spare time.

She hated to admit it, but Mom had been right. Grace *had* been shallow. She'd been swept away by Dean's looks and charm and talent, missed all the warning signs, and only discovered his mile-high stack of dirty little secrets when he'd called her from the police station to try to sweet-talk her into paying his bail. She'd been shocked and horrified, certain that he'd been wrongfully accused and outraged on his behalf. Then he'd whispered that he'd hidden enough stolen money to pay his bail behind the bookshelves in *her* apartment, and all she had to do was go get it.

She got it, all right. Accompanied by the police, plus a lawyer she'd had to spend half her savings to hire just to make sure Dean's crimes didn't get pinned on her. Her cheeks burned with embarrassment and fury at the memory.

If it had been up to her, she'd have been vague about the exact reason for the break-up, but *Promising Young Actor Arrested* had hit the papers the very next day after the phone call from hell. And more headlines had followed, finally concluding with *Formerly Promising Young Actor Gets Ten-Year Sentence.*

Grace nodded firmly to herself. Her next date might not be sexy or witty, but he'd be reliable, considerate, and honest. What she needed was a nice, plain, ordinary guy, like her mother had always told her she ought to date. A guy like her assistant, Carl.

Carl leaned over from his seat beside her and whispered, "It's 2:00 AM. Can I get you some more coffee?"

"Sure," Grace whispered back. "Two—"

"Two sugars, one cream," Carl replied. "I'll be right back."

He got up and tiptoed out of the near-empty theater. Grace watched him go. Maybe she *should* date him. He was nice. He was thoughtful. He was an excellent assistant stage manager. She'd been incredibly lucky to find someone this competent, especially considering how hard the job had turned out to be. And he seemed to like her, though he'd never asked her out.

Maybe he was just being professional, waiting for the show to open—or close, which the way things were going would probably be two nights later—rather than take the chance of mixing work and relationships. Carl was a conservative guy who didn't take risks, which, like Mom said, was exactly what she needed.

Grace imagined Carl naked.

The mental picture didn't exactly get her all hot and bothered, but she guessed he'd be… okay.

Good enough. On to step two. She imagined having sex with Carl.

That would probably also be… okay.

She shuddered inwardly. If she couldn't have absolutely fantastic, melt-your-panties sex, she didn't want any sex at all. Sex that was just okay was even more depressing than bad sex. With bad sex you could walk away sure that the next time would be better, because it couldn't be worse. With just-okay sex, you walked away thinking, "Is this as good as it gets?"

Who needed sex, anyway? She had more important things to worry about. Like her supposed big break stage managing *Mars: The Musical,* which was looking more and more like a big impending disaster. When the actors thought she was out of earshot, they referred to it as *Mars: The Mistake, Mars: The Menace,* and *Mars: The Megaflop.*

Their mistake. A stage manager was never out of earshot. Grace touched her headset. With it, she could communicate with the backstage crew and Carl. She could also hear anything going on near a headset that anyone backstage had taken off and then forgotten to switch off. Someone had once again done exactly that, so she could hear an actor doing vocal exercises and several crew members reviewing the upcoming scene shift, plus the usual footsteps, squeaks, and creaks.

"Mars!" sang the actors. "Mars!"

The actor playing Mars stepped forward. Grace hit a key on her laptop, switching on his red spotlight. Her fingers moved rapidly across the keyboard, activating more lights. In perfect time with the music, a pair of white spotlights picked out the actors representing the moons of Mars. The rest of the chorus faded into darkness.

The two moon actors began to dance around the Mars actor. One of the moon actors moved out of synch with his pre-programmed moving spotlight, so it left him in the dark and lit the floor in a white circle one step ahead of him.

Irritated, Grace hastily re-programmed the spotlight, setting it to move three seconds slower. Just as she hit the "go" button, he suddenly noticed that he was dancing in a blackout. He sped up. Now he was still in the dark, but with the spotlight trailing him like an eager dog.

"Vast space," sang the chorus. "Two moons!"

"I am Deimos," sang the out-of-step actor. "Named for terror!"

"I am Phobos, named for fear," sang the other moon actor. She was moving in perfect synch with the spotlight, but her singing was completely off-key.

The director, Lubomir, who sat on Grace's other side, muttered, "Dear God."

Grace felt for him. This was supposed to be his big break too. In the US, anyway. Supposedly he was famous in Bulgaria.

"Hey!" came a loud voice from behind them. "That's not right. You've got the orbit of Deimos moving faster than the orbit of Phobos, and it's the other way around!"

Grace turned to meet Ruth's familiar frown. The NASA consultant looked as cranky as always, her eyes bloodshot and her brown hair pulled back into a painful-looking bun. She was brandishing a calculator as if she meant to shoot a laser beam from it.

"Write down your note, and give it to me and Lubomir after the rehearsal," Grace whispered to her for the millionth time.

"But it's wrong." Ruth sounded personally offended. "I'm here to ensure scientific accuracy, and that's not accurate."

Lubomir held up his hand. "Ruth, please write down your note. Grace and I will meet with you *after* the rehearsal."

Ominously, Ruth said, "This show is funded by a grant from the National Endowment for Science Education, and the terms of the grant state that a NASA consultant must be present at all times."

Grace bit her tongue to point out that the grant only provided a small percentage of the show's budget. It was true, but they needed that small percentage. Unfortunately, it wouldn't be anywhere near enough to keep the show going if the audience hated it. Ruth might be driving them all crazy making them jump through her scientific hoops, only to have the production flop anyway.

"And here you are," Lubomir said mildly. "Present and ensuring accuracy."

"I've noted twenty-three separate inaccuracies tonight alone," Ruth protested. Flipping a page in her notebook, she said, "Number one, the Tyrrhenum cartographic quadrangle—"

"Notes *after* the rehearsal," Grace and Lubomir hissed.

Ruth subsided, scowling, and began to scribble notes. Grace couldn't usually read upside-down, but by now she'd learned to recognize Ruth's favorite note, which was WRONG. Also her second-favorite, which was MARS DOESN'T DO THAT. They were followed by a despairing scribble of WHY AM I EVEN HERE???

The actors sang on, oblivious and ignored.

Carl returned to his seat beside Grace. "Got your coffee."

She took it gratefully. "Thanks, Carl. You're the best."

He *was* considerate. Grace once again imagined having sex with him, reminding herself that he was the opposite of her evil ex and therefore perfect.

It didn't feel perfect. In fact, it made her feel vaguely nauseated.

Forget sex, she told herself. *Just focus on your job. You can't have everything, and if you have to choose between success and sex, success is better.*

But a rebellious part of her muttered, *Why do I have to choose?*

"I got coffee for you, too." Carl offered a cup to Lubomir, who took it with thanks and tossed it down in a gulp. He turned to Ruth. "The vending machine was out of herbal tea. Sorry."

"Thanks for checking," Ruth said glumly. The vending machine was always out of herbal tea.

Carl put on his headset and began murmuring directions to the stagehands backstage. "Ready to receive backdrop."

"Backdrop go!" Grace whispered to stagehands. She mentally crossed her fingers that it would all work right. The machinery controlling the stage had a tendency to jam, be late, move too fast, or make weird, un-space-like noises.

But not this time. The black flats studded with brilliant stars slid off smoothly and silently, and a huge curtain painted with a beautiful panorama of the red sands of Mars dropped neatly down from the ceiling. Black-clad stagehands emerged from the wings, placed the props and set pieces for the next scene, and vanished backstage.

Grace brought up the lights. An otherworldly glow slowly brightened on the Mars landscape, while a pair of spotlights illuminated the leading actors, Paris and Brady, who played a pair of astronauts trapped on Mars.

It was a lovely effect. At least, it would have been, except that the Deimos actor, who should have exited with the stagehands during the blackout, forgot to leave. When the lights came up, he scuttled offstage like a cockroach scurrying under a refrigerator when someone turned on the kitchen lights.

Grace sighed and took a note to remind him to leave sooner. At least Paris and Brady had managed to enter in darkness and hit the marks for their spotlights.

Paris stood poised like a dancer, with the cascade of blonde hair that Ruth was always complaining ought to be scraped into a bun tumbling down her back. Grace liked her. Paris could be a bit over-dramatic, but she was professional, always knew her lines and found her light, and occasionally brought in homemade cookies. They were good cookies, too.

Brady… Well, Brady was a typical actor. Handsome. Charming. Sexy. Flirtatious. On his fifth divorce.

He'd already dated a *Mars* actress, violinist, and stagehand, causing a three-way meltdown when he accidentally triple-booked a date and they all found out about each other. The very next day, he'd turned his charming smile on Grace and asked her out to a champagne brunch. She'd stifled the impulse to tell him to break the bottle over his head, and instead suggested that he date *anyone* not involved in *Mars: The Musical.*

Baffled, he'd replied, "But it's so convenient. We all get out of work at the same time."

Now, Brady stood in his spotlight in a long, dead silence. Finally, he turned to Paris. "Did you forget your line?"

"It's *your* line," Paris said.

"What?" Confusion was written all over his too-handsome face. "No."

"The first line's yours, Brady," Grace said, and read it to him.

As he sheepishly repeated it, she thought, *This play is doomed.* I'm *doomed.*

Grace had moved to Santa Martina to stage manage a different show. She'd thought it would be her big break. Instead, she'd gotten fired on opening night. And that was the end of her first big break.

Then she'd been hired to stage manage the play where Dean had played the leading role. That producer had been too cheap to hire an understudy, so the play closed when Dean was arrested, putting everyone out of work. And that was the end of her second big break.

Mars: The Musical was her third big break. Three strikes, and she'd be out for good.

Grace had spent her life savings on the move. If *Mars: The Musical* failed, she'd have to move back in with her parents in Delbert-by-the-Sea, Florida. Her family, who had never approved of her weird, risky career anyway, would say, "I told you so." She'd have to get some dull desk job that would bore her to tears. And to get it, she'd have to strip the dye out of her hair, hide her tattoo, and wear business suits. It would be the end of all her dreams.

It was such terrible timing, too. *Mars: The Musical* was set to open the week before Christmas, competing with a new revival of *My Fair Lady.* The two musicals would go head to head, and since most people had limited money for theatre tickets, only one could survive. Within the week, one was sure to close. And if it was *Mars*, Grace would have to slink back home for the worst Christmas ever.

And the worst life ever would follow. After her days slaving away at her boring job, she'd return to a lonely, empty home. She'd lived in Delbert-by-the-Sea long enough to know what the available men there were like. They all fell into one of two bad categories: corporate drones who disapproved of women with purple hair and creative clothing, and complete lunatics who appeared in headlines like *Florida Man Tries To Sell Three Iguanas Taped To His Bike To Passersby For Dinner* and *Florida Man Dances On Top Of Police Cruiser To Ward Off Vampires* and *Florida Man Files Patent For "Living Parachute," Ties One Hundred Giant Flying Roaches To His Suspenders, And Jumps Out The Window Of The Department Of Motor Vehicles.*

Which reminded her of another reason she didn't want to move back to Florida: the giant flying roaches. And the fire ants. And the alligators. All of which might unexpectedly invade your home. In Santa Martina, the only animals she'd seen were dogs on leashes, cats in apartments, and birds on telephone wires, and that was exactly how she liked it.

While half of Grace's mind was on her probable horrible future, the other half was watching the action onstage and listening on her headset. She could hear the backstage crew preparing for the upcoming zero-gravity scene, in which Paris and Brady would be strapped into harnesses and flown around the stage on wires. Grace blacked out the stage and watched in the dim blue set-change lights as the stagehands clipped the wires to the actors' hidden harnesses, checked and double-checked them, then hurried backstage.

"Confirm that the wires are safely attached," Grace murmured into the headset.

The backstage crew confirmed that they were.

"Confirm that you're in place and ready to pull her up," Grace said.

"In place and ready," said the crew.

Nothing seemed wrong, but something nagged at her. Maybe it was just that flying was dangerous. Grace poised her hand over the key that would bring up the lights and started to open her mouth to tell the crew to start the flying sequence.

Then she realized what was wrong.

"HOLD!" Grace yelled.

Silver glinted over Paris's head, quivering in the blue light. Despite Grace's command to stop, someone had already started pulling on Paris's wire.

Grace sprang to her feet and vaulted on to the stage. The wire attached to Paris straightened and grew taut.

"HOLD!" Grace shouted again as she threw herself at Paris, clutching the actress around the waist. "Grab her, Brady!"

At that instant, Paris was yanked into the air, violently and way too fast. She screamed. Brady flung his arms around Paris, and Grace desperately tightened her grip.

The wire pulled tight, but Paris's upward motion stopped with her feet dangling a few inches above the stage. She hung in mid-air, the wire straining above her, but Grace and Brady's weight held her in place.

"What's going on?" Paris gasped.

Grace had no time to explain. Keeping her arms tight around the actress, Grace wriggled around until she could reach the clip attaching the wire to the harness Paris wore under her costume. Grace's fingers closed on cold metal. She opened the clip.

Relieved of its weight, the steel clip rocketed into the air. The wire yanked it all the way to the ceiling, where it smashed into a light with a sound like a gunshot. Broken glass showered down. Paris screamed again, Brady ducked, and Grace flung up her hands to shield her face.

"What the hell…?" Brady began, then put Paris down and hurriedly undid his own clip. It stayed dangling in mid-air, attached to its wire.

"Nobody move!" Lubomir shouted, scrambling onstage. "What just happened? Who jumped their cue? If the stage manager says 'hold,' everything needs to stop!"

Grace, Paris, and Brady began to gingerly shake bits of glass out of their hair.

Paris stared upward, stunned. "I could have been killed."

Everyone came onstage, from the crew to the musicians to the rest of the actors. Even Ruth left her seat to peer at Paris with concern.

A chorus member said doubtfully, "The wire only flew up like that because it got pulled with no weight attached to it… right?"

Grace, Carl, Lubomir, and the stagehands shook their heads.

"No," Lubomir said. "It should never have gone up that fast or that high, no matter how much weight was on it. If Grace and Brady hadn't caught her, Paris would have been slammed into that light. She could have been seriously injured. Who rigged her wire?"

The stagehands who had set up her wire and the machinery controlling it protested that they'd done it correctly and tested it before the rehearsal.

"They did set it up right," Grace said. "I watched them. It was fine before. Whatever went wrong happened during the rehearsal."

"I watched too," Carl added. "It worked fine an hour ago."

"And why did it go after Grace called a hold?" Lubomir asked.

A stagehand shook his head. "I don't know. It flew up by itself. I never touched it."

"It's true," a chorus member said. "I was standing right next to him."

"All right," Lubomir said. "We're going to get to the bottom of this. Paris, I am so sorry. Actors and musicians, you can go home. Everyone else, we're staying until we figure out what happened and how to make sure it never happens again."

Carl touched Grace's elbow, catching her attention. "How did you know something was wrong?"

Grace had to think about it. The whole thing had happened so fast. Then she remembered what had alerted her. "There wasn't any noise. The wires always squeak a little, but they didn't this time. So I knew something had changed. I had no idea how important it was. But flying can be dangerous, so I didn't want to take any chances."

"You saved my life," Paris said. Her voice shook.

Grace felt shaken herself. Awkwardly, she said, "Just doing my job."

Ruth looked from the glass on the floor to the broken light overhead to Paris's frightened face. "That must have been terrifying. At NASA, if there's anything that could kill someone if it goes wrong, we don't just check it once. We check it hundreds of times! Thousands!"

"We didn't just check it once," Grace protested. But she could hear the defensive guilt in her voice. Considering what had happened, she *should* have stopped the rehearsal before the flying scene to run another test. The safety of the cast and crew was her responsibility, and she'd let them down.

"This is a plot!" Paris yelled suddenly, her trained voice echoing throughout the theater. "Someone's trying to kill me!"

"No, no," said a musician.

"Accidents happen in theater," said the Deimos actor. "I've never worked on a show that didn't have at least one."

"Especially in musicals," Brady added. "When I was in *Phantom of the Opera*, a wire broke during a performance and the chandelier smashed on the floor."

"Paris, I'm very sorry this happened to you," Lubomir said. "But it *was* an accident. Nobody is trying to kill anybody."

Paris was not reassured. "I'm telling you, too many 'accidents' have happened, and too many of them have happened to me! I must have a stalker. I'm not coming back here without a bodyguard!"

Grace opened her mouth to list all the accidents that had happened when Paris hadn't even been around. Then she closed it again. Why *had* there been all those accidents? It was true that musicals were disaster-prone… but *this* disaster-prone?

Maybe Paris is half-right, Grace thought. *Maybe there* is *a plot. But I don't think it's against her. I think someone's trying to shut down* Mars: The Musical.

CHAPTER THREE

Rafa

Rafa walked into the Protection, Inc. lobby. It was almost as much of a mob scene as it had been when Hal had called everyone in to tell them Ellie was pregnant. The entire team was there, apparently doing nothing but hanging out.

He turned to Hal first. "Got a new job for me?"

"No, Rafa," Hal said, sounding weary. "Not for you, not for anyone. Sorry."

Rafa glanced at the rest of the crowd. "What are you all doing here?"

Catalina laughed. "Same as you, Rafa. We had jobs we just finished. Now we're waiting for the phone to ring."

"It's like an all-predator unemployment line," Fiona remarked from the sofa.

Hal spread out his hands. "I don't know what to say. Normally I'm turning down jobs because I don't have enough agents to fill them. Just a slow day, I guess. But you don't all have to stay here. I'll call you if anything comes in."

Everyone avoided his eyes, then went back to staring at the phone.

"Guys," Hal protested. "A watched pot never—"

The intercom buzzed.

Destiny, who was closest, yelled, "Dibs!" She slammed her hand down on the button. In her sweetest voice, she said, "Protection, Inc., private security. May I help you?"

"Yes, you may," a woman replied. "Is Rafael Flores there?"

Rafa instantly recognized Paris's voice. Why in the world would she show up at Protection, Inc.? They were friends; she had his phone number. If she wanted to talk, all she had to do was call.

"I'll take—" Rafa began.

Destiny leaned close to the intercom to drown him out. "How do you know him?"

Rafa lunged for the intercom, but he was too late.

Paris's theatre-trained voice rose up loud and clear. "I'm his ex-wife."

Destiny slammed down the mute button a split second before the room erupted into exclamations and howls of laughter.

"Is this the famous twenty-four hour Vegas marriage wife?" Catalina inquired.

"Hard to say," Fiona replied with fake earnestness. "Rafa, how many ex-wives do you have, again? Five? Six? Has there been a new one since the last time I asked?"

"Fucking finally!" Nick exclaimed. "Can't wait to meet Mrs. Twenty-Four Hours In Vegas!"

Rafa glared at them all. "I was married *once,* it was a mistake—a very brief mistake—she's just a friend—Destiny, give me the intercom!"

Destiny promptly body-blocked it. Rafa stifled a groan. He should have known his teammates wouldn't give up the chance to meet the person who could give them the dirt on his infamously short marriage, which he now regretted ever having mentioned. He toyed with the idea of prying Destiny off the intercom, but she wouldn't give it up without a fight. He'd have to wrestle her for it, and that would be undignified.

With her full lips practically touching the receiver, Destiny asked, "What do you want him for?"

"Alimony," Shane said instantly.

"I want to hire him," Paris replied.

Rafa leaned over and hit the buzzer to unlock the front door, already turning over ideas about why she might want protection. She was an actress, so the most likely issue was an obsessed fan turned stalker. His annoyance at his teammates' teasing was lost in concern over her safety. That sort of stalker could be very dangerous. If she had one, he was glad she'd come to him.

Or it could be something as simple as having been cast in a movie with big stars, where everyone had personal security on the set as a matter of course, and wanting a bodyguard she knew rather than a stranger. Rafa shrugged. He'd find out what it was all about soon enough.

"Take off, guys," Rafa said. "She's just here for me."

Nobody moved. Destiny clearly spoke for everyone when she said, "Nope. We *all* want to meet her."

Gritting his teeth, Rafa went for the lobby door. He'd meet Paris at the elevator. Alone.

Nick and Fiona promptly grabbed him, one hanging on to each elbow. Shane stepped out smoothly to block the door. Irritated, Rafa tried to shake them off, but they only clung tighter. An instant later, Destiny joined them, locking her forearm across his throat as if she meant to choke him out. Catalina dove forward in an impossibly agile movement and landed lightly on her belly with her arms wrapped around his ankles. Lucas, too dignified to join in, sat back and watched, looking amused, while Hal looked on and laughed.

"Come on, guys, this is ridiculous," Rafa protested. "She'll be up here in a second. This is so unprofessional."

Nobody budged.

Desperately, Rafa appealed to his best friend, who also happened to be their boss and so had the authority to give commands. "Hal!"

Hal let out a rumbling laugh, then said, "Hands off Rafa. He's right, she's a prospective client, so we should behave professionally."

To Rafa's relief, his teammates released him. But before he could lunge through the door and slam it behind him, it opened. Paris walked in.

Everyone gawked at her. Their reactions made Rafa briefly see her through their eyes: a woman as stunning as his imaginary twin models, tall and slim and blonde and gorgeous, dressed in a fashionable yet classy style. Paris Hale, the perfect woman.

Then their eyes met, and he saw her as her real self: Paris, his old pal, whom he'd known since high school and was still buddies with, despite the very different roads they'd walked in life. Their friendship had even survived their idiotic twenty-four hour marriage. They smiled at each other.

Paris glanced around the room. She was too polite to comment on the crowd, but her carefully plucked eyebrows rose. "This must be your famous team."

Rafa forced himself to remain cool. He introduced her, giving his team his best alpha lion stare to stop them from saying anything tactless.

It worked until he got to Nick, who blurted out, "So, you and Rafa used to be married? Why'd you split up?"

"We were never really together in the first place," Paris said. "We were friends and we took a trip to Vegas, and that place can do funny things to you. Especially when there's a chapel right next to the bar."

Relieved that she hadn't revealed the awful truth, Rafa added, "By cocktail number seven, getting married by an Elvis impersonator seems like a great idea."

Everyone laughed. Seizing the opportunity, Rafa took charge of the situation. "Paris, you said you wanted to hire me. Let's go to an office and talk about it."

He took her elbow as if he was escorting her to a dance, swept her into Hal's office, and closed the door firmly behind him. It was soundproofed; everyone's voices and laughter cut off immediately.

"Sorry about the mob scene," Rafa said.

"Oh, it's fine," Paris said. "It's my fault for saying I was your ex-wife. After what happened yesterday, I was nervous about standing alone on the sidewalk, and I blurted it out because I was afraid they wouldn't let me in."

Rafa frowned, his protective lion instincts rising. "What's going on?"

"It all started when I got hired on a new show, *Mars: The Musical.* It's about two astronauts who get stranded on Mars. While they're trying to figure out how to get home, they discover alien artifacts and realize that Mars was once inhabited by intelligent life. They end up using what they learn from the artifacts to help them fix their spaceship to get back to Earth. And while they're trapped on Mars, they fall in love. So the worst thing that ever happened to them turns out to be the best—they not only survive, they find true love *and* make the greatest scientific discovery of the century. It's a really inspirational story."

Rafa smiled at her enthusiasm. "But what's the problem?"

"I think I have a stalker," Paris said.

He listened in growing concern as she recounted the series of accidents on the set, culminating in an extremely dangerous-sounding mishap involving a flying sequence.

"Has anything like that happened when you weren't in the theatre?"

Rafa asked. "People or cars following you? Strange notes left at your door?"

She shook her head. "No, nothing like that."

That was odd. Stalkers usually couldn't resist sending messages to the object of their twisted desires, declaring their love or making threats.

"Any idea who it might be?" Rafa asked. "Got any exes who didn't want to break up?"

"No. Truth is, I haven't dated anyone in a long time."

Delicately, Rafa inquired, "Trouble with the family?"

"No. They're over that by now. Last time I talked to my mother, she even nagged me about bringing someone home for Christmas." With her pitch-perfect actor's inflections, Paris imitated her mother's voice: "'Paris, aren't you ever going to settle down? Get married! You can do it now, so what's stopping you?'"

"Sounds just like my mother," Rafa said glumly. "Minus the 'you can do it now.'"

He'd never brought a date home for Christmas. Meeting the pride was something you did with your true love, not your one-night stand. He'd thought showing up alone would get easier with time, but instead, it had gotten harder. He was starting to dread Christmas, which had once been his favorite time of the year. The thought of opening that door all by himself, *again*, tied a knot of unhappiness in the pit of his stomach.

Paris gave him a sympathetic pat on the shoulder. "It's not easy, finding someone who's right for you."

"No. It's not."

He pushed aside those depressing thoughts and returned his attention to the problem at hand. Something had nagged at the back of his mind the entire time Paris had been describing the 'accidents' on the set. In the years he'd been with Protection, Inc., he'd protected a lot of people from stalkers. This didn't sound like a stalker case. It wasn't personal enough. Maybe someone was after her, but he doubted that it was a stalker. The motive wouldn't be an obsessive love turned to hate, but something else. Financial, maybe.

"Who inherits your money if you die?" Rafa asked.

"I'm not rich, you know. There's not much to inherit."

"You'd be surprised how many crimes people commit for hardly any money. Who gets yours?"

Paris looked guilty. "I'm not sure. I've never gotten around to making a will. I know I should…"

There went that idea. Paris was an only child. If she died without a will, her closest living relatives—her parents—would inherit. Her "get married in time for Christmas" mom and loving dad were hardly going to put a hit on their own daughter.

Rafa ran his hands through his mane, thinking hard. Not a stalker. Not someone hoping to inherit Paris's money, which, as she'd pointed out, she didn't have much of anyway. Then he got another idea.

"Who would take over your role if you were killed or injured?" Rafa asked.

"Melissa, the actress playing one of the moons of Mars." Paris gasped in slightly over-dramatic horror. "Do you think it's her?"

"Maybe." It seemed a bit unlikely, but you never knew. "Are you getting paid a lot for the role?"

"No. I'll get a raise if the show's a success. But I'm not in it for the money—I'm hoping it'll be my big break. So maybe she's hoping it'll be her big break instead, if she gets me out of the way."

"But only if the show's a success," Rafa said thoughtfully. "If the leading actress gets killed or has to drop out because of injuries before it even opens, that seems like it'd be likely to ruin the show's chances of ever becoming a success. You'd think she'd wait till the show's a hit, *then* try to take you out."

"Who knows what crazy things crazy people might do?" Paris said with a shrug.

"None of this seems crazy," Rafa said thoughtfully. "It seems very carefully planned, by someone who thinks they have a lot to gain."

Gain isn't just money, he thought. *What if it's not Paris's money they're after?*

What if it's not Paris *they're after?*

"Have there been any suspicious accidents when you weren't there?" Rafa asked.

She shrugged. "Got me."

"Who would know?"

"Grace," Paris said promptly. "She's there for every rehearsal, she comes in before anyone else, and she stays after everyone else leaves."

"The stage manager," Rafa said, remembering the story. "The one who saved you from getting slammed into the rafters at fifty miles per hour."

Paris nodded. "If anything weird has been going on, she'd know."

"Let's go meet her."

CHAPTER FOUR

Rafa

Rafa opened the theatre door. It was dark inside, lit only by a spotlight onstage. A man stood in the bright circle of light, singing about the beauty of outer space.

It had been years and years since Rafa had been at a play rehearsal. He'd been the star of his high school drama club, coasting on his looks, height, and confidence to make up for his merely passable acting skills. Paris, the other star, had been the one with real talent. He hoped this play would be her big break. She deserved it.

He followed her down the aisle between rows of empty seats. As his eyes adjusted to the dim light, he made out the shapes of people sitting in the front row. Paris whispered in his ear, pointing them out to him.

The petite woman with a cascade of curly hair, typing rapidly on a laptop, was "Grace, the stage manager."

The man peering over her shoulder, a tray of coffee cups in his hands, was "Carl, Grace's assistant."

The woman with her hair yanked into a tight bun, scribbling in a notebook, was "Ruth, the NASA science consultant."

The tall man in a European suit was "Lubomir, the director."

Rafa stopped in the aisle, behind Grace. With his keen shifter senses, he could hear her speaking into the microphone of her headset. Though she spoke very softly, her words were perfectly articulated and very fast. "Stand by for the set change. Stand by sound. I'm standing by on lights. On a single call, lights, sound, set…"

There was a split second of silence. Then, as the last note of the song died out, she hit a button on her laptop. "Go!"

In that instant, the spotlight blinked out, the stage took on an eerie red glow, a weird "outer space" noise sounded, and a backdrop of red sand and boulders appeared. It was all done with perfect precision, at that woman's command.

Grace seemed extremely competent. Rafa's hopes rose that she'd be able to give him a better idea of what was going on.

He folded his arms across his chest, not wanting to interrupt her work. Then he noticed another headset slung over the empty seat behind her. Rafa recalled how they worked from his high school theatre days. Put one on, and you could hear and speak to everyone wearing one.

It might be enlightening to listen in on what was going on backstage. He picked it up—engrossed in her work, the stage manager didn't notice—and put it on.

In contrast to the smooth cadence of Grace's words, a chaotic babble met his ears.

"Grace, the track for the Mars backdrops is jammed!"

"Grace, Brady says to remind you to tell the prop guy to put extra sugar in the jello he has to eat onstage!"

"Grace, the light that does the comet effect just burned out!"

"Grace, some guy's throwing up in the alley right outside the stage door!"

"Grace, I saw a rat run under Mars rock number eight!"

Rafa's mind reeled. He waited for Grace to call a halt to the scene to deal with all those problems.

Instead, she went on speaking in that same fast, soft, very clear voice: "Stand by sound. I'm standing by on lights. All stagehands not needed for the next set change, go fix the Mars backdrop track. Lights and sound, go. Tell Brady I already reminded props he wanted more sugar. Stand by to bring on Mars rock number twelve. We'll fix the comet light during the break. Mars rock go. Put a note on the stage door with a vomit warning."

As Rafa listened in amazement, he saw everything onstage unfolding smoothly, with lights shifting and sound effects happening and a red rock placed onstage. If he hadn't been wearing the headset, he'd have had no idea that anything at all was wrong.

"Stand by sound," murmured Grace. "About the rat—"

A piercing shriek made Rafa wince. It didn't come across the headsets, but emanated from backstage. "AIEEEEEE!"

An actress bolted headlong onstage, shrieking, arms flailing. "A RAT! A RAT! HEEEEEEELP!"

The actors onstage stopped singing and looked confused.

"Hold please!" Grace's voice rang out, clear and commanding. "Melissa, the rat is nowhere near you. There's nothing to be—"

"It's in my PAAAAANTS!" screamed the actress, kicking out frantically. "It's climbing up my ankle—my shin—my knee—NOOOOOOOO!!!"

A tiny furry missile flew out of her pant leg and went sailing over the footlights and into the audience. Instinctively, Rafa cupped his hands and caught it.

"Good catch, Rafa," said Paris with a chuckle. "All those years in the outfield came in handy."

"I wouldn't do that," said the woman with the notebook. "Wild rats carry rabies."

"A rat!" The actress was in full-blown hysterics, slapping frantically at her pants. "A horrible sewer rat! Filthy! Disgusting! I'll have to have rabies shots!"

Grace hit a button, and warm yellow lights illuminated the entire theatre. Rafa cautiously parted his cupped hands and peered inside them. A small white rat sat panting in his hands, its sides heaving. It was soft and furry, with tiny prickling claws. He could feel its little heart pounding, so fast that it made its whole body vibrate. But it made no attempt to claw or bite.

"You *caught* it?" came Grace's incredulous voice. "Hey, who are you?"

Still looking down at the rat, he replied, "I'm Rafa Flores. Paris's bodyguard."

"Paris doesn't need a bodyguard," Grace said grimly. "This show is what needs protection."

Rafa was still examining the rat. Clean white fur. Completely tame. This was no wild rat—someone had bought it in a pet store. And, presumably, released it backstage to wreak exactly the sort of havoc it had caused.

"Hey." It was the stage manager again. "Let me take a look."

He opened his hands a little farther.

"That's not a wild rat," she said instantly. "That's a pet. Melissa, you don't need to worry about rabies. What we all need to worry about is who let it loose."

Rafa was already smiling as he began to look up. He hadn't seen any more of Grace than the back of her head in a dark room, but from what he'd heard, she was smart as a whip and could multi-task like an air traffic controller. She'd already saved Paris's life once. Grace would be the perfect assistant to help him solve—

Their eyes met.

Mine!

The roar of his lion sounded inside his head, possessive and triumphant.

Rafa barely stopped himself from jumping in surprise. He'd been lost in Grace's beautiful eyes. They were very dark brown, and bright as black diamonds.

When he managed to tear himself away from her eyes, it was only to get lost in her other features, one by one. Her mane of curly hair dyed a rich purple that went beautifully with her olive skin. Her plump, kissable lips. Her eyebrows that arched as if she was perpetually raising them in mock surprise. Her delicious curves. The swell of her hips. The abundance of her breasts. The sweet plumpness of her legs and arms.

Her quirky punk-meets-sexy fashion sense, expressed in chunky black boots adorned with chains and zippers, fishnet stockings, a pink and white plaid miniskirt, a long-sleeved black shirt slashed almost to shreds and worn over a shocking pink tank top, and a necklace of safety pins.

Rafa knew that he was staring dumbly at her, uncharacteristically at a loss for words. But he couldn't help it. At last, long after he'd lost all hope, he'd found his mate.

Before he'd given up on the whole idea of mates, he'd always figured his would be tall, slim, and probably blonde, but definitely beautiful in the way that gets women on the cover of magazines. Traditionally feminine. Wearing a pretty dress. She'd be Paris Hale, basically, only he'd be in love with her the way he'd never been in love with Paris.

Grace Chang was the opposite of everything he'd ever imagined. Though he thought she was beautiful, it wasn't in a way that would ever land her on the cover of a fashion magazine. As for femininity, from what he'd seen of her, that scrappy little punkette had her own idea of what that meant, and it had nothing to do with tradition.

An unexpected laugh burst from Rafa's lips.

He'd been so *stupid.*

He'd thought he wanted what every other man in America wanted. And all the time, someone so much more real and vivid and wonderful than any of those imaginary supermodels was living right under his nose in Santa Martina.

The king of beasts has found his queen, growled his lion. *And oh, she is worthy of us!*

He had to make a good impression on her.

CHAPTER FIVE

Grace

Grace couldn't get over the bodyguard managing to catch the surprise!-flying rat. And without harming it, too. He not only had ridiculously fast reflexes, which made sense given his occupation, but a light touch. It was especially impressive given how big his hands were. They weren't disproportionate—he was big all over—but they looked strong enough to crush walnuts.

He was staring at her—probably wondering how a weirdo like her had managed to snag such an important job on such a big show—so she stared right back. He was strikingly handsome, with hair that made her want to run her fingers through it. It looked smooth as silk and was just long enough that strands kept falling appealingly around his face, but not so long that it looked girlish.

Grace frowned. His hair was *exactly* the perfect length. That couldn't be an accident. She knew how fast hair grew. This Rafa guy must go to the salon once a week to keep it trimmed to such tempting perfection.

Her suspicion of the sexy bodyguard grew as she continued to inspect him. He towered over her, which wasn't unusual as almost all men did, but he also towered over Lubomir, who was 6'1". Unlike the director, who always looked vaguely underfed, the bodyguard seemed made of solid muscle. His legs, his arms, his chest, even his stomach were incredibly ripped... and she could see that because he wore tight black jeans and a close-fitting shirt, clearly to show off his fabulous body. They were expensive designer brands, as were his shoes, and he wore them well. His smooth brown skin contrasted delectably with his white shirt.

She dragged her gaze from his stunning body and back to his face. Beautiful brown eyes with long thick lashes. Strong jaw. High cheekbones. Sensual lips. Everything was pure masculine perfection.

He looked like a Greek God—okay, a Latino God. And he obviously thought he was God's own gift to women.

Handsome. Rich. Cool job. Gorgeous smile, Grace thought. *This is a man to stay far, far away from.*

If Dean had been bad news, Rafa was the herald of the apocalypse.

He suddenly laughed for no reason whatsoever.

Oh, there's an imperfection, Grace thought, both relieved and disappointed. *He's a sexy lunatic.*

Apparently noticing her expression, Rafa gave her a smile charming enough to win her heart if she was weak-willed enough to let it. "You must be Grace, the stage manager who saved Paris's life last night. I've heard so much about how skilled and brilliant you are. What a true pleasure it is to meet you."

In a smooth gesture, he offered her his hand.

She didn't take it. "You're handing me a rodent."

He yanked his hand—and the white rat—back, his cheeks darkening. Was he actually blushing?

He *was.* She'd never seen a guy as manly as Rafa blush before. It was awfully cute...

Down, girl, Grace ordered herself. *He's bad news. Plus, he belongs to Paris. No way will a woman as gorgeous as her and a man as hot as him* not *end up having sex if they're together 24-7. If they haven't already started.*

Paris bent over the white rat. "Poor thing. Lucky Rafa caught it, otherwise it might have hit the back wall. Melissa's got one hell of a kick."

"Let me have it," said Ruth, putting down her notebook and stepping up. "I'll take good care of it. I used to keep rats as pets when I was a little girl."

"Rats, really?" said Paris, sounding dubious. "I used to have hamsters. So cute and furry! Not very friendly, though."

"Rats make great pets," the scientist assured her. Her usual sternness left her expression as she went on, "I'd go on walks with mine riding on my shoulder. I loved watching people do double-takes."

The hot bodyguard held out his hand to Ruth. The white rat hopped on to her palm and ran up her arm to perch on her shoulder.

"Aww," Paris remarked. "It's sweet. What are you going to name it?"

Ruth scratched behind its ears. The furry little creature gave her a sniff, its little pink nose twitching. "Tycho."

Paris laughed. "Because of the nose?"

Ruth stared at the actress. "You've heard of him?"

"I don't get it," interjected Grace.

Ruth smiled, possibly for the first time since Grace had met her. "Tell her, Paris."

"Tycho Brahe was a medieval astronomer. He got his nose cut off in a duel, and had to wear a prosthetic nose made of gold." Paris added, speaking to Ruth and sounding apologetic, "That's all I know about him. I had a pretty entertaining history teacher in high school."

"Among his many other accomplishments, Tycho Brahe measured the diurnax parallax of Mars," added Ruth. Scratching the furry Tycho's ears, she said, "It seems appropriate for a *Mars: The Musical* rat."

Grace decided not to ask what a diurnax parallax was. The last time she'd asked the NASA scientist what something was, she'd gotten a completely incomprehensible, twenty-minute lecture on orbital mechanics.

"What's a diurnax parallax?" Paris asked.

Once again, Ruth smiled. It made her surprisingly pretty. "Well, parallax is the displacement in position of..."

Lubomir, clearly registering that everyone was way too distracted for any more work to happen, called out, "Fifteen minute break!"

As everyone crowded around, Paris introduced her bodyguard to the cast and crew. He had stopped blushing by then and greeted everyone pleasantly. But Grace noticed that he kept darting glances at her. Did she have spinach in her teeth? He'd never seen purple hair before? He thought her outfit was weird?

The mystery was solved when Rafa turned to her and said, "Can you please show me around the theatre? I need to inspect it to figure out how to make it as safe as possible. Also, if you show me the locations of the 'accidents,' I may be able to find some clues."

"I can show you around," her assistant Carl volunteered.

Carl was always so helpful. But Grace couldn't help wishing that he wouldn't be, just this once. She wanted to be the one to show the hot bodyguard around. Just to look at him a bit more. That was all. She'd pretend he was a sculpture in a museum, to admire hands-off.

She was trying to think of a good reason why she rather than Carl should escort Rafa when the bodyguard said, "If Grace can be spared, I would like her to do it."

"Carl, please stand in for her," Lubomir ordered. "Grace, take your time."

Carl sat down in her seat and picked up her clipboard. "I got it."

Ruth was still explaining incomprehensible mathy stuff to Paris. The actress held up her hand, said, "Hang on, Ruth. Rafa, should I go with you?"

Grace couldn't help being impressed with the way Rafa rapidly scanned the theatre, his sharp brown eyes clearly evaluating all possible threats.

"No," he said. "You'll be safe here. Call my name if you need me."

Paris smiled and patted his bulging bicep. "Gotcha. I trust you."

Yep. They were already sleeping together. No way was a plain old hired bodyguard getting his arm petted. That was genuine intimacy if Grace had ever seen it.

She felt oddly regretful as she led him backstage. Oh, sure, she'd have to be out of her mind to get entangled with Perfect Hair Bodyguard. But it was depressing to know she'd never even had a chance. Men like him didn't date women like her. In retrospect, she was pretty sure Dean had only gotten involved with her in the first place because he'd liked her apartment better than his, and figured she'd be too busy with work to notice that he was single-handedly funding Santa Martina's stripper business.

Forcing her mind away from those gloomy thoughts, she led Rafa to the place where the stagehands worked the flying wires. He examined it closely and asked the stagehands a number of questions, then turned to Grace. "It looks like someone set up a device to pull the wire at high speed and from a distance, without anyone seeing that anything was wrong. Since the stagehands were standing right here, my guess is that it was above their heads."

He pointed upward. The ceiling was so high and full of stage machinery that any small device could have been either lost in the shadows or hidden behind something.

"Have you looked up there already?" Rafa asked.

"Yeah, but it didn't occur to me until the next day," Grace said. "By then there was nothing there."

"How many people go into the rafters? Would it be worth my time to dust for fingerprints?"

She regretfully shook her head. "A lot of people helped hang the lights and rig the scenery. Anyone could have their prints up there."

"There does seem to be a lot of touching around here." He gave a graceful wave of his hand, encompassing a chorus member giving a wire a curious poke, a stagehand on his hands and knees applying luminescent tape to the floor, and Grace herself, who was absent-mindedly straightening a set of plastic Mars potatoes on the prop table.

She hurriedly replaced the potatoes, stepped away from the table, and tripped over a stray alien artifact.

With startling speed, Rafa caught her arm, saving her from falling. "Careful!"

His hand was warm, his grip firm without being painful. It felt awfully nice to have him holding her arm…

Why hadn't he let go of her arm? She'd gotten her balance back. She jerked her gaze up to his handsome, handsome face. Which was giving her a weird, weird look. The sort of look a guy gives his girlfriend. Which was very uncool, considering that he had a girlfriend—a woman he was having sex with, anyway—and it wasn't her.

She yanked her arm away. Then she remembered to say, "Thanks."

"My pleasure," Rafa replied, his voice dropping sexily.

What was *with* him? He had a glamorous leading actress, what did he want with a chubby stage manager?

Whatever. She wasn't there to ponder the ways of hot cheating bodyguards.

Grace lifted her foot and shoved the alien artifact back to its correct place. "That's not supposed to be there. I wish people would stop messing with them. See, that's the area where they're supposed to be stored. It's very clearly marked. This is the third one I've tripped over this week. Sooner or later, someone's going to take a fall."

Rafa pointed to the place where the alien artifact had been. "Look, it was right in front of a trapdoor."

In the dim backstage light, Grace hadn't seen that the trapdoor was open. Rafa had good eyes. She bent down and closed it, then latched it in place. "Those are never supposed to be left open. We have the lights off backstage all the time. It would be so easy to fall in. Especially with a heavy prop in front of it!"

"It would, wouldn't it?" Rafa's lazy playboy air had vanished; now he reminded her of a cat on the hunt. "What would have happened if you'd fallen in?"

"I'd have broken my ankle, at the very least. Or my wrist. Something."

"And what would have happened then?"

"I might have had to leave the show," Grace replied after a moment's thought. "Once we open, I have to run the play from the stage manager's booth. You can only get into it by climbing a vertical ladder. I don't think I could do that if I had my arm or leg in a cast."

Rafa pursued the question with a relentlessness that made her understand how he'd gotten his job. "And what happens if you leave?"

Chilled, Grace said, "Carl takes over."

"How ambitious is Carl?"

"I don't know. But only Paris could have been hurt by the accident last night, and Carl wouldn't benefit if *she* had to leave."

Rafa ran his fingers through his silky black hair. "Have there been any accidents when Paris wasn't present, or that seemed targeted at someone other than her?"

"Yeah, there have." As she continued showing him around the backstage area, she gave him a rundown of every mishap that had happened to *Mars: The Musical*, culminating in a detailed account of the horrific flying incident the night before.

He listened intently, periodically asking intelligent questions. At the end, he said, "Do *you* think Paris is the target of these incidents?"

"No, I don't. I don't think any specific person is. Anyone could have tripped over that rock. And no one could have known that rat would run up anyone's pants, let alone the pants belonging to one particular person."

"Actually, they could," Rafa said. "The rat could have been trained to run up pants with a specific scent, and that scent could have been rubbed on a specific pair of pants."

Grace hadn't expected that sort of outside-of-the-box thinking from a charming hunk. Normally they coasted on their looks. But Rafa was clearly smart, as well as being hot. Muscles and beautiful brown eyes were great, but as far as Grace was concerned, intelligence was the biggest turn-on of all.

He's sleeping with Paris, she reminded herself.

Life was so unfair.

Forcing her attention back to the topic, she said, "Should we check Melissa's pants for *Eau de Rat?*"

Rafa smiled. "We can try. It might be an odor that only animals can detect, though. If that's even what happened."

"Oh, I bet it is," Grace said grimly. "Melissa is terrified of rats, and everyone in the play knows it. There's a stuffed rat we use in a lab scene, and she screamed fit to wake the dead once when it fell off the prop table. She'd thought for a second that it was a live one that had jumped off."

"Oh." He tugged at a lock of his hair again. That habit of his was driving Grace crazy. Every time he did it, she wanted to smooth back that black silk herself. "Maybe I can borrow her pants once she changes out of them. I'll take them to—" he hesitated briefly. "—to a lab. To do an analysis. They'll be back by the next rehearsal."

"That's tomorrow," she pointed out.

Again, he hesitated, then said, "I know a place that could put a rush on it."

They reached the door leading outside. Both of them stopped and stared at the note posted on it, a sheet of paper with huge letters reading, **BARF**.

"That's certainly a dramatic statement," Rafa remarked, looking amused. "But what does it mean? Is it a comment on working conditions? On the quality of *Mars: The Musical*?"

Her cheeks heated up with annoyance. "It means someone on my crew has no idea how to make a warning sign that would actually warn anyone."

"I was joking," he said hastily. "I know what it's about. I listened in over the headsets for a minute when I first came in. Do you have a pen on you?"

Grace always had a pen on her. She handed him a Sharpie. He took the sign and amended it to read,

There is **BARF** outside.

Don't step in it!

Grace, who had been ready to explode with fury, laughed instead. "Thanks. Well, the BARF is one thing I can't blame on whoever's trying to sink *Mars: The Musical*. There's a bar next door."

He gave her a thoughtful glance. Quietly, he said, "Is there somewhere a little more private where we could speak?"

"Sure." She indicated a built-in ladder leading straight up the wall. "Come into my booth."

Grace climbed up first. When she was halfway up, she glanced down to make sure he was following her. He was, his long arms and legs making easy work of the rungs. And, she realized, he was getting a fantastic view up her skirt.

She scrambled up the last few rungs like they were on fire.

Once she was in her booth, she smoothed down her skirts and sat in her chair, trying to seem dignified. Rafa climbed in, glanced at the low ceiling, and, in a fluid movement, managed to slide into the chair beside her without ever standing upright.

"I'm impressed," she admitted. "Most people hit their heads on the ceiling the first time they come in."

"Most people should have the common sense to look up when they climb into an attic," Rafa remarked. His sharp gaze swept around the booth, taking in Grace's station between the light and sound boards, the snarl of cords and plugs beneath them, the headsets, and the huge window with its view of the stage. "When do you move up here?"

"A couple nights before we open. Right now it's easier for me to be in the audience, so I can physically get onstage and backstage if I need to."

"Lucky for Paris that you could. So, what do *you* think is going on?"

She hesitated, eyeing him warily. "I have a theory, but everyone I've told it to has thought I was crazy."

Rafa stretched out in his chair, crossing his ankles. He was a blissful island of relaxation in the middle of the chaos that was *Mars: The Musical*, and those legs of his seemed to go on forever. "Let's see if I can break that streak. Hit me."

"I think someone's trying to shut down *Mars: The Musical*."

It was at least the fifth time she had said that sentence. But the response she got was one she heard for the very first time. Rafa nodded and said, "I think so too."

"You do?" She couldn't believe it. "Everyone else brushes me off when I say so."

"No wonder this has gone on so long. Who benefits if the show fails or never opens?"

Grace had to think about that. She'd been so caught up in trying to convince people of her theory, which she'd spent over an hour trying to explain to the cast and crew the night before, that she hadn't had a chance to think of its implications. But once she did, she realized there could only be one answer. "*My Fair Lady.* It's the other musical opening at the same time. If *Mars* doesn't open at all, or if opening night is a disaster and it gets terrible reviews, everyone will see *My Fair Lady* instead."

He tipped an imaginary hat to her. "Congratulations. You've solved the mystery. Watch out, you'll put me out of business."

She couldn't help feeling warm inside at his words. It really was too bad he was Paris's guy. She'd enjoyed talking to him. Sitting so close to him that she could feel the heat of his body. Gazing at his gorgeous brown eyes. His charming smile. The place where his shirt had pulled up to expose a bit of his washboard abs…

Stop it.

"So, someone from *My Fair Lady* must have snuck someone into *Mars* to sabotage it, right?" Grace asked. "Any idea who?"

"Not yet, but we'll find out," Rafa assured her. "And in the meantime, I'll shift from protecting Paris to protecting you."

She stared at him. "What makes you think they're after *me?*"

"I mean, protecting the show in general," he said quickly. "Which includes you. I just mentioned you because you're the one I'm talking to."

She didn't quite follow that explanation, but she saw a bigger problem than that. "Won't Paris mind?"

"Not once I explain that she's not the only target. And I'll still *also* be guarding her. But in the meantime, since I won't need to escort her around outside of the theatre… May I take you out to dinner on Saturday night?"

For a single, golden moment, Grace was delighted. Of course she wanted to go out with this hot, smart, strong, intriguing hunk—a hunk who wanted to know her opinion about things and took it seriously once she'd told him. When had she ever met a man like that? Never, that was when.

Then bitter disappointment crashed over her as she remembered that he was already taken. Rafa was nothing but a smooth, charming cheater, like all smooth, charming men. How could she have been fooled by him, even for a moment?

CHAPTER SIX

Rafa

Grace's expression had told Rafa everything he needed to know: she *did* like him too. She'd looked delighted when he'd asked her out. But then the happiness lighting up her face vanished, to be replaced with disappointment, hurt, and anger.

"God! Isn't Paris enough for you?" she demanded.

Rafa instantly realized the misunderstanding. *He* knew what his relationship with Paris really was, but he also understood what it must look like from the outside.

"She and I are just friends," he assured her.

"Really," she said, with a clear subtext of *bullshit.*

"Really. We're close, sure. But it's because we're old high school buddies. Look into my eyes, Grace, so you can see I'm telling the truth." He stared hard at her, making sure she could see his conviction. With complete honesty, he vowed, "Paris and I have never been romantically involved."

For a brief and shining moment, he was delighted to see his one true mate finally, *finally* stop eyeing him with the deepest suspicion. On the contrary, she gave him a grin, full of relief and camaraderie.

"Oh," Grace said. "OH! Okay, then. In that case, I'd love to go out with you."

And that was the moment when Rafa remembered that he and Paris had once been *married.*

He suppressed the urge to go and bang his head against the wall.

All else aside, it was adorned with mangy old theatre posters where it wasn't speckled with mold. And he hated getting blood in his mane.

What the hell had he been thinking?

That you and Paris were never in love, replied his lion, with the distinct subtext of *you idiot.* Loftily, as if he was addressing a toddler, he went on, *That you never courted each other, longed for each other, or made truthful vows to each other. And, most importantly, that you do not pine for her now.*

That explanation is not going to fly, Rafa retorted. *What happens when Grace finds out that Paris is my ex-wife?*

Nothing, if you tell her right now, said his lion. *Go on.*

Rafa opened his mouth to do so. And then another horrible realization fell on him like a ten-ton cement truck.

He had *two* difficult explanations to make, not one. At some point he'd have to reveal that he was a shifter. She couldn't be one herself, or she too would have known at first sight that they were mates. So he not only had to explain that he was the ex-husband of the woman he'd just said he'd never been romantically involved with, he also had to claim to be something people thought didn't even exist. He'd not only seem like a liar, he'd seem like a lying lunatic.

Grace was still smiling, her purple hair glinting like amethysts in the beam from an overhead light. She looked absolutely radiant at the prospect of going on a date with him. He couldn't bear to do anything to wipe that smile from her face.

He couldn't tell her now. It was too soon. They'd only just met. He'd wait, court her like she deserved to be courted, build up a solid basis of trust and love, and *then* tell her, when she'd be more willing to hear him out.

Yes. That was the only possible option.

But he couldn't help feeling like he'd already made a catastrophic, life-ruining mistake.

Grace, still beaming in a way that made him feel 50% blissfully happy and 50% like the floor was going to crumble beneath his feet at any second, said, "I have to get back down. Want to come with me, or do some more detecting from up here? You can listen in backstage with the headsets."

"Just listen?" Rafa asked. "You don't have closed-circuit cameras?"

She shook her head. "Wish we did. Maybe we'd have caught My Fair Villain by now."

"I'll install some tomorrow."

"I don't think we can afford them," Grace said regretfully. "Maybe I could get Lubomir to spring for one nanny cam."

"A nanny cam's not a bad idea." He looked down at the stage. The fifteen minute break had ended, and the actors were rehearsing again. For all he knew, the mystery villain was backstage, hidden from sight, busy as a bee with a very vicious sting. "Don't mention it, though. The saboteur's more likely to strike on camera if he or she doesn't know they're being filmed. If we haven't caught them before opening night, I'll put in a real system so you can watch what's going on backstage from here."

"Sounds good." She got up. "So, are you coming?"

"Yeah. I need to take Paris aside and explain that I'll be guarding everyone, not just her." And while he was at it, he could also explain the list of words he didn't want her to say. Such as "Vegas," "married," and "24 hours."

He followed Grace down the ladder and into the audience.

Her assistant Carl was speaking softly into a headset, like she had been earlier, but was clearly struggling. "Stand by sound—no, sorry, not yet—ask me later, I'm on stand by—go! Go! Yes, sound go! No, set change is still on stand—sets go!"

Carl hit a button. Lights brightened onstage, but not where the actors were. Their singing faltered as they were plunged into darkness. He hurriedly hit another button, bringing the lights up on them, and muttered a curse.

Grace tapped him on the shoulder, put on his headset, and slid into his seat. She began to speak as smoothly as if she'd never stopped. "Stand by sound. Stand by scene change. How many of the alien artifacts are missing? Sound and scene change… Go!" She hit a button, adding a red glow to the lights. "Okay, substitute Mars potatoes for the missing artifacts so Brady will still have something to pick up. Stand by…"

The sound of her voice was hypnotic. Rafa could have listened to her all night. He was only distracted when someone cleared his throat.

It was Carl. "Would you like some coffee?"

"Sure," Rafa said absently, most of his attention still on Grace as she arranged for one of the stagehands to sneak onstage during a blackout to warn Brady that Mars potatoes would be standing in for two of the alien artifacts. "Cream and sugar, please."

Rafa sat down behind Grace and beside Ruth. Tycho the rat was still perched on the NASA consultant's shoulder. Both of them were intently watching the scene onstage.

Ruth wrote in her notebook, THERE HAS NEVER BEEN INTELLIGENT LIFE ON MARS!!! Her pen punched through the paper on the third exclamation point.

The lights came up onstage, revealing Brady carefully excavating one small, fossilized machine and two shimmering blue potatoes from a lump of red clay.

"An alien artifact!" Brady exclaimed. Then, with a wink directed at the audience, he ad-libbed, "And alien potatoes. Yum!"

Grace glared at him and muttered, "Catch me ever warning you again."

With a soft, despairing moan, Ruth wrote, THERE ARE NO POTATOES ON MARS EITHER!!!!

Her little white rat gave her ear a consoling nibble.

Paris came onstage. "Alien artifacts? I knew it!"

The musicians struck up a wistful tune as Paris began to sing. Grace made the lights change to a beautiful outer space effect, with twinkling stars shining on the stage floor.

"Somewhere out there

Somewhere up there,

There is wonder," Paris sang.

"Wonder," echoed Brady.

The actors playing moons emerged and danced around them as Brady brandished an alien artifact in one hand and a blue potato in the other, and Paris sang about how she'd always believed in impossible things.

"At least the song admits they're impossible," Ruth muttered. But she didn't sound unhappy. In fact, Rafa could swear a little smile hovered over her lips as she listened to Paris sing. Paris did have a beautiful voice.

As Paris belted the final note, she flung her arms out wide in a dramatic gesture. Her tight silver jumpsuit ripped from collarbone to belly-button.

She let out a shriek so loud that Rafa was surprised that no glass shattered, then flung up her arms to hide her breasts. Brady jumped and dropped the potato. It ricocheted into the lights at the edge of the stage. *Then* glass shattered.

"HOLD!" Grace and Lubomir shouted.

"I need stagehands to clean up broken glass," Grace added into the headset. "And a replacement for footlight number nine. Please tell wardrobe that Paris's spacesuit tore and needs to be sewn back together, ASAP."

Grace ran onstage, followed by Ruth.

"I can tape the suit together," Grace said, waving a roll of silver duct tape.

"Or you could borrow my coat," offered Ruth, pulling it off. "Here, take it."

Paris smiled at them both. "Thanks, but I think I'll just go backstage and change into my street clothes."

Two stagehands hurried onstage with a dustpan and broom, and began sweeping up the glass. A third came in with a replacement light. Brady went to retrieve the Mars potato.

Rafa felt a huge grin spreading across his face. He hadn't been involved in theatre since high school, with the exception of going to Paris's plays. But he'd only watched those from the audience and congratulated her afterward. Now he remembered how much he'd enjoyed the camaraderie and teamship that came from actually working on a show. Despite the outsize egos, melodrama, and ridiculous mishaps, everyone always ended up becoming a sort of found family by the time the show opened.

If Rafa hadn't found the same bonding through shared effort in the face of seemingly impossible odds, first in the Navy SEALs and later with Protection, Inc., maybe he would have stayed in theatre. And then maybe he'd have met Grace earlier, and saved himself all those years of loneliness and unsatisfying one-night stands and having to make up way more one-night stands than he'd actually had. Not to mention his twenty-four hour disaster marriage.

But it had all worked out. He loved the job he had. And now he *had* met Grace. Everything he'd ever wanted was within his grasp. All he had to do was make sure she didn't find out about his Vegas marriage until he found the perfect time and way to inform her, make sure she didn't find out he was a shifter until he found the perfect time and way to inform her, court her the way she deserved to be courted, catch the *Mars: The Musical* saboteur, and save the show. All in time for Christmas, so he could take her home to meet his pride.

Piece of cake, purred his lion. *We are mighty.*

"Fifteen minute break!" Lubomir called belatedly.

Paris headed backstage, now with Ruth's coat buttoned on top of her spacesuit. Rafa leaped up and followed her. He didn't like the thought of her venturing backstage by herself, before he got the nanny cam installed. And it would be the perfect opportunity to talk to Paris alone.

He kept a careful lookout for trip-wires, open trapdoors, and other booby traps as he escorted he, but there were none. Maybe the theatre gremlin was done for the night.

Paris opened the door to the tiny dressing room crammed with costumes and makeup mirrors. "Turn your back."

"Of course." Rafa turned around, closed the door, and kept his eyes fixed on it. "Let me catch you up on what I've figured out so far…"

He quickly explained his theory and that he wanted to guard the whole show, not just Paris. She didn't object. He hadn't thought she would.

"I'm glad, to be honest," she said. "It's pretty scary to feel like someone's trying to kill me specifically. And I was nervous that someone else might get hurt in a trap that was meant for me. Now that you'll be guarding everyone, I actually feel a lot safer."

"There's something else," he began.

Inexplicably, his heart started pounding. That was strange. He was a lion shifter, the king of beasts, not to mention a former Navy SEAL. Nothing scared him. But all he'd done was *think* of the possibility that his secrets would ruin the relationship with Grace that he didn't even have yet, and he was overwhelmed by a horrifying sense of impending doom.

"You can turn around now," Paris said. "What's up?"

He turned. She had shucked off her ripped spacesuit costume, and was now sitting in front of a makeup mirror in the same dress she'd worn to Protection, Inc., with Ruth's coat over one arm.

Rafa hesitated. Close as they were, he had never told her that he was a shifter. For the protection of all shifters, that had to be kept a secret from anyone but your mate. Which meant that he couldn't say that Grace was his mate. That was awkward.

"Do you believe in love at first sight?" he asked.

"Nope," Paris replied immediately.

Even more awkward, growled his lion. *Say something smooth. Quickly!*

"Well… I do," Rafa said.

His lion let out a growl of despair at his total lack of smooth.

Shut up, Rafa told him. *This is Paris. She doesn't care.*

Trying to ignore his lion's annoyed rumblings, he went on, "At least, I do now."

Paris, quick to catch on, stared at him, then grinned. "Seriously? Who is it? Melissa? One of the musicians? It's the oboe player, right? She's really beautiful."

"It's not the oboe player. It's Grace."

"No way!"

Irritated, Rafa said, "She's much prettier than the oboe player. Hotter, too. Much hotter. And it's not just her looks. I've seen her in action, and she's incredibly quick-witted. Funny. Assertive. Hard-working. And I don't know if you've noticed, but she has a terrific body. Her legs alone—"

Paris's laugh cut him off before he could continue listing his mate's virtues, though he hadn't even come close to running out of them. "Oh, I'm not arguing. Grace is fantastic. I didn't think she was your type, that's all."

"Neither did I," Rafa admitted. "I suppose that's why it took me so long to find her. I've been looking in all the wrong places. Anyway, I don't want to screw this up. Does anyone here know about our Vegas thing?"

"Nope."

"Good. Don't say a word about it. I want to explain it to her myself."

Paris rolled her eyes at him. "Of course I won't say anything. But you better explain it ASAP, or it'll look like you've been lying to her. And you really don't want her to find out on her own."

"There's no way that could happen. You're the only one who knows about it. And yeah, I'll tell her soon." He couldn't bring himself to confess his idiotic claim to Grace that he and Paris had never been romantically involved. Why had he blurted that out? It made his inevitable explanation so much harder. "Thanks. Oh, and when I do, is it all right with you if I let her know the entire story? I'll tell her not to repeat it."

Paris considered it, her head cocked and her blonde hair bright under the makeup lights. "Yeah, it's fine. Honestly, I'm tired of keeping secrets. I guess I'm just looking for the right time to let it all hang out."

"Me too."

She smiled at him. "Love at first sight, huh? It's funny, I've been in so many plays where that happens, but I've never seen it in real life. I've always thought love is something that sneaks up on you over time."

"I think it is for most people." Most people who weren't shifters. "Just not for me."

"Lucky you. Though I kind of like the sneaking up."

Paris brought a bag with her when they went back. Carl returned at the same time, with coffee for everyone.

Rafa accepted his with thanks, noting that Grace too drank hers with cream and sugar. It was a tiny, silly thing that they had in common, but noticing it made him feel good. It was something that they shared. He watched her full lips sip her coffee as he drank his own, imagined how soft they would feel on his own, and felt like all was right with the world.

"Herbal tea?" Ruth asked hopefully.

Carl shook his head. "Sorry, the machine's broken again."

"HA!" Paris's trained voice shook the rafters. With a flourish, she reached into her bag and pulled out a thermos. She unscrewed it and poured steaming liquid into a cup, which she handed to Ruth. "I hope you like chamomile."

The scientist's face lit up. "My favorite! How did you know?"

"I'm psychic," Paris replied, then grinned. "No, I heard you asking Carl, back when you thought that machine was going to start working at any moment."

Ruth sipped her tea with a deep sigh of contentment. "Give me a cupcake, and I'd die happy."

"What's your favorite type of cupcake?" Paris asked.

Ruth glanced around guiltily, as if admitting to some secret crime, and admitted, "Chocolate. The richer the better. I know it's not healthy…"

Paris gave an airy wave of her hand. "Everyone needs a vice."

A brilliant idea leapt into Rafa's mind. Paris had sometimes baked cookies for the cast and crew of their high school plays, and he bet her skills had only improved since then. "Grace, what's your favorite cupcake flavor?"

Grace also looked slightly guilty. "I like the, uh, unusual ones. Lavender, Captain Crunch, red licorice, that sort of thing. I know, I'm weird."

"You're *quirky*," Paris said kindly.

Rafa caught Paris's eye and tried to telepathically signal to her, *Can you make unusual cupcakes for my love-at-first-sight? I'd do it myself but I don't know how to bake.*

Paris apparently understood, or at least understood the *please bake unusual cupcakes* part, because she winked and gave him a little nod.

"What about you, Rafa?" Grace asked. "What are your cupcake needs and desires?"

The way her voice got a little throaty as she said "needs and desires" instantly plunged him into an incredibly vivid fantasy of her asking him, "What are your needs and desires?" while they both lay naked in bed.

No, while he lay naked in bed while she knelt naked atop his hips, so he had the best view of her luscious breasts. He could practically feel the weight of her soft thighs. Maybe he'd have scattered red rose petals across the sheets, so their sweet perfume rose up and mixed with Grace's own natural scent—

Grace snapped her fingers. "Earth to bodyguard. Favorite cupcake?"

Rafa's mind went completely blank. It was like the image of Grace naked had melted it down. Finally, floundering, he said, "Rose?"

He immediately cursed himself. That wasn't even a real flavor, *and* it wasn't manly. A man presents a woman with a bouquet of roses. He doesn't make them into cupcakes and eat them himself. He was opening his mouth to take it back and claim that he loved some other flavor, any flavor, when Grace replied.

"Hey, I like rose cupcakes too. You're the first person I've ever met who doesn't think they taste like soap. High-five!"

She held up her hand. A little dazed, Rafa smacked it. Her hands were just as soft as he'd thought. Well, he certainly wasn't going to say he didn't like rose-flavored cupcakes now. And also, he was *definitely* putting rose petals on the bed the first chance he got.

Paris polled the rest of the cast and crew on cupcake preferences, and then Grace and Lubomir called them all back to work. Brady returned to the stage, where he gave a suspicious prod to a wobbly red thing resting on a squiggly green thing.

"What's that supposed to be?" Rafa whispered to Grace.

"Martian food," she whispered back. "It's strawberry jello in a... Martian shape. On a Martian plate."

Brady sliced into the Martian jello with a squiggly green knife, then popped a bite into his mouth with a squiggly green fork. An expression of disgust came over his face as he chewed and swallowed.

"Grace!" he bellowed.

She sighed. "What's wrong with it this time?"

"Too much sugar," replied the actor.

"Didn't he say he wanted more sugar?" Rafa whispered.

"Yep," Grace whispered back. "He's like Goldilocks on Mars: this Martian jello is too sweet, that Martian jello is too sour. Except he never finds the Martian jello that's just right." To Brady, she called out, "I'll tell props to put in less next time."

She was much more patient with Brady than Rafa would have if he'd been her. But then, that was what made her good at her job.

Much as Rafa would have liked to spend the rest of the rehearsal sitting beside her, enjoying her warmth and voice and presence, there had been enough mishaps—or sabotage attempts—that he decided to divide his time between the audience, the stage manager's booth, and backstage. He made sure that he wasn't dividing it evenly, so no one could predict when he'd show up backstage. But he didn't catch anyone doing anything worse than secretly swigging from a flask (the conductor) or carving obscene graffiti into the bottom of a Mars rock (a bored stagehand).

There were no more "accidents" for the rest of the rehearsal. But Lubomir wasn't happy with one of the main song-and-dance numbers, in which the entire chorus came out dressed as Martians to act out Paris's fever dream while she was lost and dehydrated on Mars. The rehearsal ran overtime, but finally ended.

The actors and musicians changed into their street clothes, then left.

They were followed by the light and sound people, and then the stagehands. Rafa took the opportunity to grab Melissa's rat pants. Once he was alone, he'd shift and sniff them. His lion might be able to catch a scent undetectable to humans.

Lubomir, Grace, and Carl discussed a problem with the sound effects. Grace said she'd stay to fix it. Carl offered to help, but she told him to go home and get some sleep. He left, along with a yawning Lubomir.

At last, Grace and Rafa were alone in the theatre.

They stood looking at each other. Heat seemed to fill the air between them. Rafa was certain she could feel it too. The chemistry between them was electric. He knew that if he reached out to pull her in for their very first kiss, she would melt into his arms.

He was about to do it when he remembered his secrets. Should he tell her before they did anything at all, even kiss? But they'd known each other for such a short time. Maybe it was too soon…

She took a deep breath, then swallowed. "I better go work on the sound board. You don't have to stay."

"Of course I'm staying," Rafa said instantly. "I have to protect you."

"From deadly wires and jacks?" Her tone was light, but she gave an uneasy glance around the mostly-darkened theatre. "Well—all right. If you don't mind not getting much sleep tonight. This could take a while. And it'll be pretty boring."

"Spending time with you? I doubt that."

They walked together to the ladder.

"Ladies first," said Rafa.

"Uh-uh." Grace shook her head, making her purple curls swing, and gave him an unbearably sexy wink. "You got to stare at my ass last time. My turn now."

"With such a classy invitation, how can I refuse?"

"You can't. That's why I don't do subtle." She snapped her fingers. "Go on. Give me a show."

He took his time climbing the ladder, grinning to himself. She certainly knew how to keep him on his toes. He loved her boldness. And if she wanted to get a good look at his ass, well, she was absolutely welcome to it. She could ogle any or all parts of him, clothed or nude, any time she liked.

The stage manager's booth was very small; Grace moved easily within it, but Rafa had to be careful not to hit his head on the ceiling or knock anything over with a careless move. And though the rest of the theatre was cool, it was hot, both because heat rises and because it had a lot of machines in a confined space.

Grace indicated two control panels built into a pair of tables, with as many switches and dials as an airplane cockpit. "Those are the light and sound boards. Sound's the one with the problem. It's been acting up a lot. It might be best for me to rewire it from scratch."

Rafa vaguely recalled stage managers from high school. They had usually been the people from the drama club who'd tried out for roles they didn't get, and ran around looking harried and resentful. He definitely didn't recall them doing any electrical repairs.

"How'd you get to be a stage manager?" he asked. "Do you have to go to school for it?"

"I think most of us learn on the job," she replied. "You start out as a stagehand, then become an assistant like Carl, then a stage manager."

"But how did you know it was what you wanted?"

"I always liked tinkering with things. When I was five, my parents gave me Malibu Barbie and her pink Corvette. I took them both apart and put them back together into a freaky cyborg vehicle with hands and feet and long blonde hair."

Rafa laughed.

Grace grinned at him, then went on, "When I was in high school, my shop teacher recommended me to the drama teacher. I started out setting up the lights, and then she asked if I'd like to run them, and then she asked if I'd like to run the whole show. I said sure. She said I'd need to be assertive. I said, 'No problem.' I was an outcast in high school, and I liked the idea of being able to order all my classmates around."

Rafa's amusement at Monster Car Barbie vanished at his anger that anyone, even immature teenagers, had shunned her. How dare they!

"I'd thought of being an engineer before that," Grace said. "But once I tried stage management, it was love at first sight. I've never wanted to act or sing or anything like that, but I love taking a huge production with tons of moving pieces and making the whole thing run perfectly."

"This show has a ton of moving pieces, all right," Rafa remarked. "Actors… Mars rocks… Rats…"

Grace chuckled. She had an incredibly sexy laugh, low and throaty. "Hopefully there won't be any more rats. But yeah, this is the most complicated show I've ever worked on. I'm from a little Florida town called Delbert-on-the-Sea, and even commuting into the nearest city, there wasn't much work for a stage manager. I came here to get my big break."

"And here it is. *Mars: Mission Accomplished.*"

She gave him a wistful smile. "I sure hope so. The thing is, this isn't the first time something's seemed like my big break. I moved to Santa Martina to stage manage a different show. It was supposed to be my big break, but it turned out to be a big bust."

"Another musical?"

"No. It was an extremely serious play about alcoholism, *The Bottom of the Bottle*. The sort of serious that tips over into accidentally funny. It had this ridiculous dream sequence where a bunch of actors came out dressed up as beer cans…"

"In a serious play about alcoholism?!"

"Yep," Grace said, grinning. "They grabbed the star and wrapped him up in black leather straps. It was supposed to represent how he was imprisoned by his addiction, but it looked more like he was seriously into bondage. They put him in a black leather harness, which made the whole thing seem even more like a scene from *Fifty Shades of Grey*, and suspended him from the ceiling. Just like we do in *Mars* for the zero-gravity scenes, actually, only for no good reason. He dangled overhead like an S&M spider while the beer cans marched around him in a circle, chanting, 'Chug! Chug! Chug!'"

By the end of the story, Rafa was laughing so hard that tears came to his eyes. He wiped them away. "I can see why that theatrical masterpiece wasn't your big break. Did it close after opening night, or last an entire week?"

"Believe it or not, it's still running. What happened on opening night was that I got fired."

"What?" Rafa couldn't believe it. "Why?"

"Opening night sold out," Grace said. "I guess there's no accounting for taste. After we'd sold out, people were still showing up and asking for tickets. The producer said, 'Let's move in some folding chairs, and sell tickets for those!' But that's illegal. It's a fire hazard. I took him aside and explained why we couldn't do it, and then I went to double-check the equipment for the flying scene."

"Uh-oh. And while you were gone…?"

"You got it. He had a row of folding chairs blocking the fire exits, and a row perched on a high ledge without a rail, so if the person sitting in them leaned back too far, they'd flip over backward, fall ten feet, and land on cement. Probably on their head."

"Holy shit."

Grace nodded in grim agreement. "I went to the producer and told him I was getting rid of those seats. He said, 'Touch them and you're fired.' I said, 'It's my duty as a stage manager to protect the safety of everyone involved in this show, and that includes the audience.' I started folding up the chairs. And he fired me. Had my assistant run the show. No one fell over backward and the safety inspectors didn't do a surprise check that night, so he got away with it."

"He was lucky." Inside Rafa, his lion was snarling in fury. "And he was an asshole. He fired you for doing the right thing. Some day that'll come back to bite him."

"It might. It's a pretty popular show. I keep wondering if he's still bringing out the danger chairs every time it sells out. Some day his luck will run out. I just hope no one gets killed."

"You could try anonymously tipping off the safety inspectors," Rafa suggested.

Grace gave him a slightly guilty grin. "I have, actually. So far they haven't caught him in the act. I know it's not my problem…"

He recognized the sound of someone repeating what they'd been told rather than saying something they actually believed. "Who said that?"

"Everyone who I told about calling the safety inspectors after I left the show. It was my responsibility while I was stage managing, but afterward, I guess it just seems like I'm a busybody and a control freak and trying to get revenge." Her bright smile flashed. "I mean, I'd *also* like to get revenge. But even if it does make me nosy and vengeful, I still don't want some unsuspecting audience member to crack their skull. Or to have them trapped if there was a fire."

"What it makes you is an honorable, responsible person who cares about other people," Rafa said. "You're like me: you want to protect people. That's a good quality! The world would be a better place if more people were like you."

Grace stared at him as if she couldn't quite believe what he'd said. She was silent, but her eyes took on a liquid shine. Had he actually made her cry just by saying that she was a good person and had done the right thing? Hadn't anyone ever told her that before?

She swallowed and blinked. In a slightly husky voice, she said, "And more people were like you?"

"Well, of course."

She chuckled, as he had hoped she would. Then she gave a wistful glance down at the stage. "I really like this show. I know you've only seen it in bits and pieces, but it's a lot of fun, the music's catchy, and it's visually spectacular. I hope it's a hit. I'd love to keep working on it. But even if it wasn't much good, I'd hate for it to fail. If it does, I have to go back to Delbert-on-the-Sea. I just don't want to have to give up on my dream."

"You won't," Rafa assured her. "I'm sure it'll be a hit. But even if it isn't, you're too tough to give up forever. It'd be a setback, that's all."

"A long setback," she said glumly. "It took me years to save enough money to come here."

"Still not forever. But like I said, I *don't* think it'll flop. What I've seen of it looked great. And I'm here to make sure the sabotage stops."

To himself, he vowed, *I'm here to make your all your dreams come true.*

"Thanks. I'm sure you will. I bet the theatre gremlin took one look at you and fled in terror." Grace glanced at her watch. "Whoa, time flies when you're going on and on about yourself. I better get started on the sound board."

She took out a toolbox, plunked herself down on the floor, and wriggled under the table.

"Told you it'd be boring," she said, her voice muffled. "You won't be able to see anything but my legs."

"You say that like it's a bad thing," Rafa returned. "But is there anything I can do to help? Pass you tools, maybe?"

"I don't know. Can you fit?"

He surveyed the tight space below the table. "Let's see."

Rafa crouched down. He unbuckled his belt and took off his gun, then placed it where he'd be able to see and reach it. The booth was too small for him to lie flat, like Grace was doing, so he bent his legs back, flattened his chest to the floor, and slithered under the table.

"I'm impressed," Grace remarked. They were crammed so close together that he could feel her warm, sweet breath on his face. "I didn't think a big guy like you would be able to squeeze under here."

The question is, can we squeeze out? his lion remarked pessimistically.

"I got in—and out—of much tighter places than this in BUD/S," Rafa said. Automatically, he began to explain, "That means Basic Underwater Demolition—"

"Whoa!" Grace exclaimed. "You were a SEAL?"

"Yeah. My boss now was my best buddy on our team. When Hal and I were done with the SEALs, I helped him found Protection, Inc. Hey, how come you know what BUD/S stands for?"

"I just love reading Navy SEAL romance novels." Her voice dropped to that throaty register again, making Rafa feel slightly dizzy. And also glad he was lying on his stomach, because otherwise he'd be rudely prodding her with the biggest hard-on of his entire life.

"You do?" Rafa managed.

She laughed. "I'm kidding. One side of my family has a lot of people in the military. Mostly Navy, though I have a cousin here in Santa Martina who's an Army vet. No SEALs, but I have an uncle who tried and didn't make it."

"Did he get into BUD/S?"

"Yeah, but he got injured in Hell Week and had to drop out."

"That's pretty good," Rafa said. "Most people don't even qualify for the training."

She squirmed around to give him a curious look, which pushed one of her legs into his. "What percentage of the ones who do get in make it through?"

"Uh…" It was hard to think of anything with her warm, soft body lightly touching his. He felt like he was about to spontaneously combust. "About twenty percent."

"So, if about twenty percent qualify, and only twenty percent of them pass, then the percentage of everyone who becomes a Navy SEAL is… I swear I know how to calculate that… It's impressive, anyway. I'm impressed. Man, it's hot in here." She took a deep breath, which pushed her *breasts* into him.

Rafa's head swam. Was she doing it on purpose? She had to be doing it on purpose. Right? Normally he could easily follow women's cues, but something about Grace got to him. Made it so he couldn't think straight.

"Do you... Do you want me to...?" As Rafa heard his stumbling voice, he wanted to kick himself. Where was his suave? What woman would respond to *that?*

"Yes," Grace replied fervently. "I do."

His lion roared in triumph.

CHAPTER SEVEN

Grace

For a big man crammed into a tight space, Rafa moved with incredible agility. The instant she said, "I do," he'd somehow caught her up in his arms and clasped her tight. For a split second, she was amazed and impressed that he'd managed it without smacking his or her elbow or head into anything.

And then his lips met hers, and she stopped thinking of anything at all. She only *felt.* The incredible strength of his arms around her, holding her tight and safe and warm. The silky strands of his hair falling around her face. The heat of his mouth. The wild passion of his kiss, like nothing she'd ever felt before.

She melted into him, trying to press every inch of her body into his. There was no part of her that didn't want to be touched by him. And to touch him. His skin was so smooth over the hard muscle it covered. She slipped her hands under his shirt, caressing his back and chest. When she toyed with his nipples, she felt as well as heard his indrawn breath of pleasure.

"No fair." Rafa's voice was hoarse. "Yours are all covered up."

"Gotta do something about that." Grace heard her own voice crack.

She began to wriggle out of her long-sleeved shirt, rolling it up over her sides. He helped her slide it over her breasts, then over her head and off. It was quickly followed by her tank top.

That left her bra. Which, she realized with regret, wasn't one of her sexy satin or lace bras, but a gray cotton sports bra that covered up nearly as much as her tank top.

"If I'd known I was going to strip under a table, I'd have worn something nicer," she said. "Or at least something *less*."

"Are you kidding?" Rafa replied, and beneath the joking she could hear the hunger in his voice. "You're the best Christmas present ever. Half the fun is in the unwrapping."

He neatly unsnapped her bra, then slipped it off her shoulders.

There was a brief silence, broken only by the sound of his breathing. She'd never seen a man look at her like Rafa was looking at her, like she was the most precious and desirable woman in the entire world. When he cupped her breasts in his hands, it was reverence as well as lust. He started teasing her nipples, making them contract into taut little nubs, and then she couldn't look at him any more because her eyes had closed of their own accord.

She felt for him, found his mouth, and kissed him hard and greedily. He responded with a passion to match her own, his muscles tensing with his sharp inhale. He wanted her just as much as she wanted him, she could feel it, and that only made her hotter and hungrier. And all the while, his fingers never stopped moving over her breasts, never stopped sending shuddering ripples of delight up and down her spine.

Grace lay in the heated dark, trembling with pleasure and conflicted desires. She wanted him to go on stroking and caressing and fondling her breasts forever *and* she wanted him to reach a little farther down *and* she wanted to unzip his pants and—

Rafa reached a little farther down. She drew in a breath as his fingers slipped into her panties and rubbed her sensitive clit. Her hands clenched on the bulging muscle of his shoulders, harder and harder as the waves of pleasure washed over her, building and building until she was gasping and panting and digging her nails into his skin with the power of her climax.

An eternity later, she opened her eyes. Rafa was holding her, breathing as hard as she was, his black hair hanging in sweat-damp strands and his dark eyes hot with desire. The air was like steam all around them, suffused with an enticing masculine musk. Grace should have been done, but she just wanted more. And he hadn't had anything yet.

She dropped her hand down, and found the right spot just as easily as he'd found her clit. A huge, steel-hard erection thrust into her hand.

She grabbed it and squeezed.

"Oh, God," Rafa groaned—or maybe *growled* was a better word.

He shoved his hand into his jeans pocket. She felt him fumbling for what felt like ages before he withdrew it, condom in his fingers and triumphant gleam in his eyes. "Got it! If you want it."

"Of course I want it. You get it open. I'll get *you* open." She put her hands on the button of his jeans.

"That might be hard," Rafa said. He clearly had no intention of making a joke, and looked startled when she laughed. Then he joined in, a little raggedly. "In more ways than one."

He was right. She struggled with the button—his jeans were pulled so tight, she was surprised they hadn't ripped—and finally managed to get it open.

Rafa gave a sigh of relief as she unzipped his jeans. "That's better."

He helped her shove his jeans and boxers down past his hips. His cock was just as big as the rest of him, and pressed against her belly like a steel rod.

She rolled down her panties. They were still half-clothed, with his shirt and her skirt on, but there was no way she was going to wait long enough to fully undress to get him inside her. That would feel like an eternity of tortured longing. They'd gotten rid of the clothing that would be a barrier, and that was all they needed to do.

"Now, Rafa," she said. "Put it in me now!"

"I love a woman who knows what she wants." His voice dropped to a husky purr that made her even more desperate. If she didn't get him inside her right now, she'd lose her mind.

He wrapped his arms around her and slid into her with a single thrust. She arched against him, moaning. It felt so good to have him inside her. So delicious. So *right.*

Rafa gave a soft little growl with every thrust, a noise that sounded just as satisfied as she felt. There was something about him that reminded her of some great cat. A lion, with that incredible hair of his, even though it was black rather than blond. Something primal and untamed.

"Come on," she heard herself muttering, and didn't know if she was talking to him or to herself. "Come on. Come on—"

Pleasure flared within her, brilliant as a sunburst. She was still floating on it when she felt Rafa come, his growl now loud and fierce.

They lay still, spent and happy and close together. She laid her head on his shoulder. There was something so comforting about the solid muscle of his body. It made her feel like she was perfectly protected. She probably was. After all, he was a bodyguard. He protected people for a living.

Rafa stroked her hair. How could a big tough bodyguard like him have such a gentle touch?

How could she have ended up under the table with a guy like him? Rafa was handsome, sexy, strong, funny, competent, sweet, *and* obviously not at all turned off by a woman who used tools and ordered people around for a living.

Was he too good to be true?

Or was he her *real* big break—the perfect man for her?

"I love—" Grace hurriedly closed her mouth on *"I love you."* Where had that thought come from? It was ridiculous. Way too soon. The heat and the mind-blowing sex must be making her delirious. "Uh, I loved *it.* Yeah. Fantastic. Has anyone ever told you you're great at sex? Forget it, I'm sure everyone tells you that, and honestly I don't want to know about the everyones. I'm sorry, I'm babbling. Pretend I didn't say anything."

"I'll pretend you didn't say anything but 'Fantastic, you're great at sex,'" Rafa said with a grin. "And by the way, so are you. That was the best sex I've had in my entire life."

"Yeah, right," she couldn't help muttering.

He cupped her face in his hand. His hands were so big. But not disproportionate, he was just a very big guy. Big all over. She had never cared one way or another about height or bulk, but Rafa's great big hands were incredibly sexy. So were his great big muscles. And his great big—

"Hey. I'm not handing you a line. It's the truth. I love—" Rafa broke off. "Uh, I loved it too. Come on, do you think I faked my orgasm?"

Grace couldn't help laughing. "No. I didn't fake mine, either."

"So, we're agreed," he said easily. "Best sex ever. We should do it again some time."

"How about right now?" she suggested, then shook her head. "Wait, no, we can't. I still have to rewire the sound board."

"Sure. I've got your tools right here." He stretched out his arm and tapped her tool box.

"Let me get dressed first. No way am I using a soldering iron topless."

"That would make a great pin-up calendar," he teased. "'Sexy Stage Manager Strip-Solders!'"

Grace wriggled out from under the table, then watched incredulously as Rafa extracted himself with athletic ease.

Navy SEAL, she reminded herself. *Top 1% or whatever at getting in and out of tight spaces.*

All the same, it was very impressive. And she loved watching him move, with his catlike agility and sensual flex of muscle. It was hard to tear her gaze away, especially when he was so deliciously disheveled, with his shirt untucked and his pants pushed down and his hair falling all over his face. He looked like the living embodiment of sex.

He reached back under the table and handed Grace her clothes, which she put on while he disposed of the condom in the nearest trash can, thoughtfully hiding it under an avalanche of coffee cups.

As she leaned over to adjust her skirt, he reached out, pushing her hair back on one side. "Hey, I missed seeing that before."

She knew what he saw: a butterfly tattooed behind her ear, and the words, *fly free.* "I got it for my eighteenth birthday."

Rafa touched it. Once again, she was amazed by the delicacy of his strong hands. "It's very you. I like it."

"Thanks. And now I really am fixing the board," Grace said reluctantly. "If you come along, all you're going to be doing is handing me tools."

She slid back under the table. Rafa followed. Just as she'd asked, he did nothing but pass her whatever tools she requested. He did stay very close to her, but it wasn't as if he had much of a choice, and she sure wasn't going to object. It was nice not to have to work alone, and even nicer to work with assistance from a sexy guy who, bizarrely, seemed perfectly content to lie there and watch her solder wires.

The time flew by. Finally, she was done. She wriggled out from under the table, stretched, and yawned. Rafa followed her out, his eyes as bright and his demeanor as energetic as it had ever been.

"Thanks for letting me help," he said.

"You weren't bored?" Grace asked.

He shook his head, sending his sleek hair flying. "I have a teammate, Shane, who's an amazing martial artist, and I love watching him practice. I have another teammate, Fiona, who's an undercover specialist, and I love watching her get into character. Watching you fix that board was like that."

Grace's eyes stung with unexpected tears. She looked away.

"I'm serious," Rafa protested.

"I know you are." Grace heard her voice come out thick and choked. Normally she hated showing that kind of emotion in front of people. But something about Rafa made it feel all right. "It's just that most people think it's weird for a woman to be good at this sort of thing. Lots of men literally don't believe me when I tell them what I do."

"Show me those idiots, and I'll break them in half for you," Rafa snarled. Grace stared at him, her mouth open. He sounded like he meant it. "Women command ships in the Navy. Women serve on submarines. There's women on my team, and I trust them with my life. As for your job, well, you don't strip wires with your balls."

She snickered. "I would hope not."

His brown eyes seemed to spark as he went on, "What exactly is their problem? They're such knuckle-draggers themselves, they think women aren't evolved enough to use tools?"

That made her grin. "Basically. But it's not just that I work on mechanical and electrical equipment. It's that I give orders, and a lot of the time I have to do it fast, so there's no time to say 'please' or 'thank you.'"

"I don't want anyone bothering with 'please' or 'thank you' when there's bullets flying," Rafa remarked. "Even metaphorical bullets. I've heard you over the headset. It is literally impossible for you to say 'please' for everything."

"And I work too hard and I care too much about my career and I'm too driven. For a woman. Anyway, that's what they say," she concluded.

"*I'm* driven," Rafa pointed out. "I work hard. I care about my career. Same with everyone who's ever gotten through BUD/S. And everyone on my team. And everyone who ever succeeds at anything. You don't need a dick to work hard, but if you put people down for doing what you're too lazy to do yourself, then you *are* a dick."

Grace swallowed. "Thanks. That means a lot to me."

"This isn't just about work, though, is it?" He sounded cautious, as though he was stepping on glass. "Someone specific did something to you."

"Yeah. My ex." Grace hesitated, knowing the rule about not discussing exes on a first date. But Rafa had asked, and in a way that made it obvious that he'd drop it if she didn't want to talk about it. So she gave him the briefest possible explanation of Dean and how he'd lied to her, cheated on her, and ended up in jail.

"But the worst part was that he wouldn't let it go," she went on. "He kept calling and emailing me and insisting that I wasn't being fair to him and he could explain and I had to give him one more chance. He just would not respect me telling him not to stop contacting me. I had to change my email and phone number to get rid of him."

A protective fury burned in Rafa's eyes. "He's lucky he's in jail where I can't get to him. But you let me know if you ever hear from him again. I promise, it'll be the last time you do."

"I will." Grace felt warm inside hearing his promise, and seeing that he didn't blame her. And it was good to know that he wasn't the type to refuse to take no for an answer. "Do you have little sisters, by any chance? You seem like the big brother type."

"I do. Two of them. But I also have big sisters. Two of them, too. I grew up with a lot of strong women. My mom, my grandma, my aunts, my sisters. In my—my family, it's traditionally the women who—the women who are strong." Rafa broke off, looking irritated, though she got the sense that he wasn't annoyed at her, but at himself for tripping over his words. He'd sounded like he'd meant to say something else entirely.

Family secrets, she thought. Grace didn't press him on it. Every family had some.

"Anyway, I lo—I like the woman you are. Driven. Hard-working. Giving orders. Organized. Smart. Good with tools." With a wicked smile, he added, "Good with your bare hands, too."

"You're not bad yourself. Hey—be a gentleman? Walk me to my car?"

"But of course." Rafa managed a seated bow, and even one which looked elegant rather than ridiculous.

He escorted her to her car, clearly keeping a lookout for bad guys, and kissed her before she got in. It was all she could do to not drag him inside for a backseat quickie.

As she drove through Santa Martina's darkened streets, she thought, *Rafa really is a great guy. Why* shouldn't *I get a man who's handsome, fun, sweet, sexy, and crazy about me? It's just my own insecurities telling me it can never work out.*

But that insecure part of her wouldn't shut up. In a voice like poison, it whispered, *What about Paris? If they're really not romantically involved, why* did *she pet his arm like that?*

Too good to be true.

CHAPTER EIGHT

Rafa

As usual, Rafa woke to an empty bed. But unusually, the feeling of his long limbs stretching out and touching no one didn't bother him. Instead, he was filled with contentment. He'd finally met his mate!

He folded his arms behind his head, as relaxed as if he was stretched out on a sunny savannah, and leisurely recalled every moment of making love with Grace. It was a memory he'd treasure forever. And as long as he avoided any catastrophic screw-ups, he'd have an entire lifetime of new memories to create with her.

Energized by the thought, he scrambled out of bed and took a shower. Recalling that Grace had seemed to like his tight white shirt and black jeans of the day before, he selected blue jeans (to make sure she didn't think he was one of those same-clothes-every-day guys) and another tight white shirt. She'd also seemed to like his hair, so he took special care with it. Then he scooped up Melissa's pants and headed to Protection, Inc.

He'd tried shifting and sniffing them the night before, but he hadn't caught any unusual odors. But lions hunted by sight, not scent. While his lion's sense of smell was better than his man's, it was nothing compared to what a wolf or bear could do. He needed to enlist Hal or Nick. Preferably Hal. While Nick's wolf had the best sense of smell out of the entire team, Nick the man had no tact whatsoever. If he noticed that Rafa looked unusually happy, he'd want to know why.

Rafa didn't intend to tell his teammates about his mate just yet. It wasn't because they'd tease him. He was a big boy—he could take it. But they'd demand to meet Grace, then haze *her* to make sure she was worthy of him. Sure, he'd hazed his teammates' mates, but it was different when it came to Grace. She could undoubtedly handle it, but she shouldn't have to.

He wouldn't say one word about his mate until he'd had a chance to head off the hazing at the pass. When the time was right, he'd reveal Grace to his team, just like he'd reveal his lion and his former marriage to Grace. If being a Navy SEAL had taught him anything, it was that no mission was impossible, so long as you planned it carefully and executed it with finesse.

Filled with confidence, Rafa strode up to the Protection, Inc. lobby and flung open the door. There was a yell, a crash, and a thud as the door banged into something and bounced back at him.

Cautiously, he pushed open the door, only to be confronted by an overturned chair and Nick's hot green glare.

"What the fuck?" Nick snapped. "Watch where you're going!"

"I walked in the front door of my own workplace," Rafa pointed out. "It's not usually barricaded."

Nick dusted off his black leather jacket, then righted the chair. "I was hanging a picture."

"Should've waited and asked me," Rafa suggested. "*I'm* tall enough to put it up without having to stand on a chair."

Nick gave him another good glare. "Whatever, man. Enjoy your extra two inches and monkey arms."

"Three inches," Rafa corrected him, then took a look at the picture Nick had just hung on the wall.

All the members of Protection, Inc. had photographs of themselves in their shift forms hung in the lobby—even Lucas, who was shown circling the skies above his ancestral palace, the sunlight glittering off his dragon's golden hide. Rafa's photo had been taken on a family vacation, with his pride lounging on an African savannah. The newest member, Catalina, had recently put up her own shot, of a lithe leopard climbing a towering redwood tree.

Nick's old photo, which was now on the floor, was of himself at the head of a wolf pack chasing a deer in a forest. The one he'd hung in its place was of his wolf in the snowy woods outside of Santa Martina, his eyes bright and alert. But though Nick was alone in the new photo, he didn't look lonely. His intense gaze was fixed on the unseen person taking the picture.

"Did Raluca take that shot?" Rafa asked.

"Yeah. How'd you know?"

Rafa couldn't tell him the truth: that he now understood how people felt when they looked at their mates, and he'd seen it shining out of the gray wolf's eyes. He shrugged. "She's your mate. It's the obvious guess. She's a good photographer."

Proudly, Nick said, "Raluca is fucking awesome at everything she does. She's going to be the best fashion designer ever."

"Maybe she'll give you a makeover," Rafa teased. "I hear pink is the new black."

Nick didn't rise to the bait. Touching Raluca's gift to him, a starkly hewn silver dragon coiled around his forearm, he said, "If she gives me something pink, I guarantee you it'll look fucking badass."

Rafa gave up. Nick was probably right, anyway. "Is Hal around?"

"Nope. Just me."

Rafa considered waiting for Hal to return, then decided against it. Nick *did* have the best nose of any of them. And he hadn't noticed Rafa's found-my-mate glow, so it probably wasn't that noticeable.

Rafa took Melissa's pants out of a bag. Before he could say anything, Nick said, "They're not your color."

Rafa didn't dignify that with a response. "Do me a favor and smell them? I think someone might have put some kind of scent on them."

Nick took the pants and sniffed.

"I meant as a wolf," Rafa began.

Nick tossed back the pants. "Don't need to. You're right, they're scent-marked. Someone sprinkled them with vanilla."

"Huh. I'd have thought I'd have been able to smell that myself."

"Just a tiny bit," Nick said with a shrug. "Not enough for anyone but a werewolf to pick up. So what's this about?"

Rafa explained, leaving out any mention of Grace.

By the end of his story, Nick was laughing. "The big cat catches the rat! Well, call me if you need any more help sniffing or whatever. I'm taking off. I have to pick up Manuel at the airport."

Rafa's ears pricked up at the mention of Manuel. He'd once delivered the kid to an airport himself, back when Nick had been the alpha of a werewolf gang and Manuel had been its youngest member. "How is the kid?"

An alpha's pride lit Nick's eyes as he said, "He's doing great. Loves his new pack, and they love him. Loves college, and his professors think he's a fucking genius."

"Is he here for his Christmas break?"

"Winter break, yeah. He'll fly back to spend Christmas with his pack, but he'll be here for a while. He's crashing with me and Raluca. I'll bring him to see the team, of course. I know he wants to catch up with you all. But don't call him a kid. He's almost twenty."

Rafa tucked "don't call him a kid" away for later teasing purposes, as he did with anything that annoyed Nick, and asked, "What's he majoring in?"

Nick shrugged. "Hasn't decided."

"Still?"

"He's got another six months to make up his mind," Nick said, instantly leaping to his former packmate's defense. "You don't have to declare your major till the end of your sophomore year."

It was always mildly surprising to Rafa when he heard phrases like "declare your major" or "sophomore year" come out of Nick's mouth. The street-smart werewolf had grown up with no contact with college (other than maybe spraying graffiti on one) or college students (other than maybe mugging some). But once an alpha, always an alpha. If something was important to a member of his pack or even a former member, then Nick would learn about it.

Just like Raluca had gone to college and there discovered a gift for clothing design, and suddenly Nick was throwing around phrases like "fashion-forward." Or rather, being Nick, "fashion-fucking-forward."

Rafa wondered what new interests *he'd* develop because Grace cared about them. Theatre, obviously. Musicals, maybe. Electrical equipment. Unusually-flavored cupcakes.

A pop startled Rafa. Nick had snapped his fingers under Rafa's nose.

"What?" Rafa asked, jolted back to his senses.

"I said, 'See you!'" Nick shook his head reprovingly. "Man, you're spacey today. Get some sleep before you go back on the job."

He sauntered out, the old photo under his arm. Rafa folded Melissa's pants, made a mental note to pick up a bottle of vanilla to test the rat-attractor theory, and headed for the tech room to collect a nanny cam.

When he opened the door, he saw the room with new eyes: Grace's eyes. He'd been telling the truth when he'd said he'd loved watching her fix the sound board, and it had been not only because of her obvious competence, but because of her even more obvious enjoyment of the work.

When he brought her to the tech room, he was sure she'd love both the cutting-edge devices and the oldies but goodies. To her it wouldn't be a mere repository of useful stuff, it would be a Wonderland and a playground. And most of all, he bet, she'd love the handful of gadgets Fiona had designed or remodeled.

No, what she'd enjoy most of all would be meeting Fiona herself. Not only would Grace appreciate a woman who knew her way around wires and microchips, but Fiona was another woman succeeding at a male-dominated job. They had so much in common.

As if his thoughts had summoned her, Fiona looked in. She was dressed to kill in a spectacular black gown with silver accents and black silk opera gloves. Her white-blonde hair, which she usually kept braided and coiled atop her head like a crown, fell loose, flowing all the way down to her hips.

"Hi, Rafa. What're you looking for?" Then her sharp green eyes narrowed. "*You* look happy. What's up?"

"Do I usually look miserable?" he parried.

"You don't usually look like you're walking on air. Found another set of twins last night?"

"Nope. Triplets," Rafa shot back. "*Identical.*"

She laughed.

Before she could pursue the interrogation further, he jumped in to deflect her. "What's up with the outfit? Are you on your way to an undercover job?"

"No, an opera matinee."

Fiona liked musical theatre! Sort of. Grace *would* love her.

"What are you doing here, then?" Rafa asked.

"I needed to pick up some ammo. I didn't have anything small enough for this at home." Fiona twitched aside a fold of the gown, revealing a discreet slit in the fabric and a tiny pistol strapped to her thigh.

"What's going on?"

"Nothing." She shot him a look like he was the weird one for asking. "I never go anywhere unarmed. Do you?"

"Sure. I only carry when I'm on the job."

There was a brief silence in which Rafa was sure he and Fiona were thinking the same thing: *all this time working together, and I didn't know that about you.*

Come to think of it, there was a lot he didn't know about her. Which was strange, given how long he'd been on a team with her. Hal had planned Protection, Inc. when he and Rafa had been Navy SEALs, and Hal had brought Destiny on board before they'd launched the agency.

Fiona had been Hal's first recruit after they'd started. But Rafa had never gotten the whole story of how Hal had found her or what she'd been doing before. Hal had said not to ask and that she would tell him eventually. But she never had.

"Fiona, has Hal given you a new job yet?"

She shook her head. "Got something for me?"

"I hope *My Fair Lady* isn't too much of a come down from the opera. Because I need someone to look into it…"

He outlined the sabotage of *Mars: The Musical* and his theory that someone from *My Fair Lady* was behind it. He felt guilty for omitting Grace's heroism and cleverness from his account, but he had to leave her out entirely. Fiona picked up on subtext much better than Nick did. If Rafa so much as said Grace's name, Fiona would figure it all out.

When he finished, Fiona nodded. "No problem. I'll do some spying on *My Fair Lady* and keep you posted."

"Thanks."

He selected a nanny cam from the surveillance equipment, and then they walked out together. After they parted ways at the parking garage, Rafa drove first to a market to buy a bottle of vanilla and a few other things, then to a florist's to buy a dozen bouquets of red roses. Then he drove home and installed the roses in vases around the bed, along with an array of candles, and arranged the final bunch of roses in a vase in his living room.

He made sure he had a lighter for the candles, bottles of red and white wine plus an excellent champagne, romantic music, and of course condoms. Also some scented oils. Silk scarves, useful for bondage or blindfolds or simply rubbing over skin. And so forth. He had everything his mate might desire, whether her tastes ran to the simple or the elaborate. Much as he'd enjoyed their tryst under the table, he knew that women appreciated romance, and he wanted to give his mate the best a man could offer.

When he brought her home, he'd escort her to the living room, offer her a glass of whatever she wanted (he'd also bought a selection of sparkling fruit juices in case she didn't drink), then duck into the bedroom to scatter rose petals over the bed and light the candles.

Later, when they were cuddling in the afterglow, he'd introduce the topic of getting to know each other better, and so naturally lead into telling her about those goddamn twenty-four hours in Vegas.

Possibly also about shifters. He'd play that part by ear. But he felt confident that he'd be able to reveal Big Secret Number One in a way that would not lead to conflict or heartbreak or anyone running away screaming, and had an excellent shot at getting Big Secret Number Two out of the way at the same time, also without conflict or heartbreak or anyone running away screaming.

Nothing could go wrong.

CHAPTER NINE

Rafa

Rafa arrived at the theatre well before the rehearsal was scheduled to begin. He'd meant to wait in the parking lot until Grace arrived, then escort her inside. But when he pulled up, he saw that her car was already there.

He hurried inside, his heart pounding. He shouldn't have assumed anything about what time she'd arrive; he should have asked for her plans, then arranged for them to meet. He hated the thought of her being alone in the theatre. Or, worse, not alone.

"Grace!" His shout echoed in the empty theatre, amplified by the high ceilings.

"Hey, Rafa." Grace's voice also echoed; he couldn't place where it was coming from.

Then a familiar head of purple hair rose up from the floor, soon followed by the rest of her as she climbed out of the trap door. Rafa ran to greet her. He took a moment to enjoy her outfit of the day—a black beret, an oversize black sweatshirt with a geometric pink pattern, a black lace skirt, sky-blue socks, and black platform boots—before he swept her up in his arms.

"You look great," he said.

"So do you," she replied. "So don't take this as a complaint, just as curiosity. Do you ever wear anything but jeans and a T-shirt? I mean, they're very nice jeans and T-shirts, but…"

"Why, do you want to give me a makeover?" Rafa returned. "Tonight

I'm taking you to one of the best restaurants in Santa Martina, so I could wear a suit. That is, if it goes with what you're wearing. If you want to stay in this, probably I should stay in mine, so we'll match. Sort of."

She gave him a speculative look, as if she was mentally dressing him up. "Hmm. I think I'll change into something more conservative. I bet you look good in a suit."

You look like the king of the urban jungle, his lion assured him.

"When you see me in it, you'll have to tell me if I do or not." He took Melissa's pants, the bottle of vanilla, and the nanny cam out of a bag. "The pants were scented, all right. With vanilla, of all things. I hope Ruth brings the rat back. If she does, we can see if it was trained to go to anything that smells like vanilla."

Grace sniffed the pants. "I still don't smell anything. Did you take them to the lab?"

Don't lie to your mate, growled his lion.

Just one tiny little one, Rafa thought uncomfortably. *After tonight, I'll never lie again.*

"Uh… yes." Well, he could hardly say he'd had his teammate smell them. But he still felt guilty. He hefted the nanny cam. "I'll set this up now."

"Need any help?"

"No," he began, then realized that he probably did. "Actually, yes. Come with me and make sure I'm not putting it where it'll get lit up or cast a shadow during the show."

They went backstage, where she directed him in setting up the concealed nanny cam. He put the monitor in her booth, where he or she could check it periodically during rehearsals and watch it constantly once the show opened. Though he hoped he'd catch the saboteur before then.

She stayed backstage so he could make sure it was working. He sat in her chair in front of the light board and watched the monitor as she wandered about backstage, straightening props and checking the flying wires. The nanny cam was working perfectly. He was about to leave it and come down when he saw her stop and look straight into the camera. Her expression sent all the blood in his body rushing into his cock—and that was *before* she leaned over, reached under her skirt, and pulled off her panties.

He was torn between leaping up and rushing backstage, and staying where he was so he wouldn't miss a thing. Paralyzed by those choices, he remained in the chair as if he was glued to it, watching on the monitor as she slowly removed her boots and socks. The boots had so many buckles and zips that it took a while before both of her feet were bare.

She had the daintiest little feet. Rafa wanted to kiss them.

The beret followed. Then the sweatshirt. This time she was wearing a sexy bra, a scrap of black lace fine as a wisp. She stood still for a moment, letting him get a good look at her luscious breasts nearly overflowing from the bra, before she unsnapped it and lifted it from her shoulders.

There she was, naked from the waist up, barefoot, wearing nothing but the lace skirt. Which, he remembered, had nothing underneath it.

And then she took off the skirt.

Blood thundered in Rafa's ears. He'd never seen anything so hot in his entire life. It wasn't just the strip tease, though that was *incredibly* hot. It was her daring. Her inventiveness. Her desire to please him. Her desire. She wasn't a shifter but she was wild enough to stalk the savannah, a bold woman who saw what she wanted and grabbed it in both hands.

Rafa took one last, long look through the monitor, then jumped up. He banged his head hard on the low ceiling, but he didn't give a damn. He had to get down there to his mate. It was killing him that he wasn't touching her already.

How he managed to get down the ladder rather than just leaping off the edge, he didn't know. He scrambled down in record time, then bolted backstage.

She was still standing there, alone amongst the Mars rocks and tables of props and racks of costumes. Naked. Her nipples were brown-pink and fully erect, and he thought he could catch a glimpse of glistening wetness between her thighs.

"Took you long enough," she remarked. But though her tone was light, he caught the huskiness in her voice. She was having trouble controlling herself, too.

He bent her back and kissed her hungrily, his hands roaming over her curves. She responded with passion, her hot tongue stroking his.

He could feel her breasts heaving against his chest, the hard nubs of her nipples pressing through the thin cloth of his shirt. Her scent of some light perfume and her own arousal surrounded him.

Some distant part of his mind wondered if she'd locked the doors or if anyone might come in at any moment and catch them. But he couldn't bring himself to stop kissing her for long enough to ask. She was writhing against him, her hands clutching at him under his shirt. He was so turned on, he couldn't think of anything but the caress of her hands, the soft warmth of her skin.

He wanted to bury himself inside her, right now. But he wanted to make her come, right now, even more. He *had* to feel her arch and hear her cry out, and to know he was the one giving her that irresistible, almost unbearable pleasure.

Rafa dropped his hand down, pushing it between the pillowy curves of her thighs. She shifted her weight, opening herself to him. His fingers touched liquid heat and petaled folds. She moaned into his mouth as he sought out her clit, and gasped as he found it. The tiny button was swollen with arousal and, he could tell by her reactions, exquisitely sensitive. Her slick juices ran over his fingers as he played with it and in the responsive areas around it, and the musky scent of her increased.

He loved feeling her tremble and stiffen in his arms as he sought out the height of her pleasure. Some other time, he'd prolong it. But now, as she thrust herself into his hand, he couldn't hold back. Her walls clenched around his fingers as she came with a shuddering cry.

Grace relaxed, seeming to melt into his arms. She seemed satisfied. But Rafa wasn't. And not just because he hadn't come yet. Her striptease had been so exciting and erotic, he wanted to give her something as thrilling in return. He waited till her breathing and heartbeat steadied and she was standing by herself, then dropped to his knees before her.

He glanced up and saw her gorgeous brown eyes widen.

"Really?" Grace's voice was beyond husky and into rough. He loved the sound of it. That was how far he'd brought her. "You're gonna go there?"

"Don't you like it?" he asked.

"Oh, I like it!" Grace said, and he could hear how much she meant it. "I just thought—I mean, you haven't—"

"I'll get mine. Later. This is for you."

"Oh, just for me, is it?" A teasing note lightened her voice. "You're not getting anything out of it yourself?"

This close, her scent was overwhelming. It made his head swim. "Maybe a little bit. But I'll try really hard not to let it get to me. Don't want to come in my pants or anything."

"You try hard, then." But when he bent his head, she held up a hand to stop him. "Wait. Give me a second to take a mental picture. You look really good down on your knees. Your shoulders—your hair—me naked and you still dressed—"

She shook her head, clearly running out of words. Rafa smiled. He'd thought she'd like that. And if she liked just looking that much, how much pleasure would she get once he really got going?

"Okay," she said at last. "Go for it."

Rafa once again bent her head, and this time he tasted her. He felt as well as heard her sharp inhale, tasted the sweet tang of her, felt her folds part beneath his questing tongue. The muscles in her thighs jumped as he breathed out over her sensitive clit, then gave it the most delicate of licks.

"Oh, God!" Grace gasped.

Her hands came down on his shoulders and gripped him tight. He let their pressure tell him whether to go light or hard, gentle or forceful, when to stop and press a kiss into her inner thigh, and when to bend to her once again. Her excitement delighted him. He loved sensuality, loved sex and his mate's body, loved giving and getting sexual pleasure, loved thinking up ways to thrill his mate. And now he had a mate who clearly loved all those things just as much as he did.

He loved *her*—loved her so much that it made his heart seem to swell inside his chest.

She was gasping steadily, her pulse throbbing, her walls beginning to contract. He closed his lips over her clit and sucked gently, and she writhed against him and let out a short, sharp scream as she came.

He stood quickly so he could wrap his arms around her and let her rest her head against his shoulder.

"Wow," she murmured after a while. "You are incredible."

"So are you," he replied. Then he suddenly remembered something. "Did you lock the doors?"

That question jarred her out of her dreamy post-orgasmic haze. "Yeah, but Carl and Lubomir have keys." She glanced around the theatre, then pointed. "There. That closet."

They stumbled into it. The closet was fairly roomy, as far as closets go, but Rafa was big enough that it was still a tight fit.

"Hold on," he said. "I'm not sure I'll have enough room to get undressed once you close the door."

He was far too desperate to bother stripping down in the sensual way that she had done for him. He took off his belt and holster and laid them aside, then kicked off his shoes and roughly hauled off his pants and shirt, only pausing to yank a condom out of his pocket. Within seconds, he was as naked as his mate.

She rolled the condom on. The touch of her fingers made him start and gasp. Even the lightest pressure felt almost unbearably intense.

"Now you know how I felt," Grace remarked.

She slammed the door, leaving them pressed together in the heated dark. Even with his sharp lion's vision, he could see nothing. He had only his other senses: hearing, scent, smell, touch. The lack of sight heightened them to an incredible intensity. He could hear and feel even the slightest movements she made. Her enticing scent surrounded him. He could still taste her. It drove him wild.

Rafa linked his hands beneath her hips and scooped her up. He didn't need her excited whisper of "Go on" to know she was ready. With a single thrust, he sank himself deep within her.

Nothing had ever felt as good as sheathing himself in her tight wet heat. He felt half-mad with pleasure as he drove into her in a hard, fast, powerful rhythm. Though he couldn't see her, he could hear her gasps and feel her legs wrapping tight around his back, and he knew she too was being carried toward an unstoppable climax.

It was pitch black inside the closet, but his orgasm made him see stars.

He had to brace himself to keep standing; he felt weak at the knees. More than that, he had to bite his tongue not to say, "I love you."

Say it, growled his lion.

Not yet, Rafa silently replied. *When the time is right.*

He set her down. They leaned against each other, panting and sweaty and satisfied.

"What time is it?" Rafa asked.

"No idea," Grace said dreamily. "But we should have time to get dressed before anyone else shows up. Probably."

"Who's the usual early bird?"

"Might be Lubomir. But it's usually Carl."

How embarrassing and awkward for Grace if her own assistant caught her naked! Rafa couldn't let that happen. "Let's go!"

They burst from the closet, a broom falling out in their wake. She snatched up a dusting cloth, which they used to dry each other off with, then tossed it back into the closet, along with the broom. He disposed of the condom, and they dressed in record time.

Grace was still zipping up her boots when Rafa heard the backstage door open. He went to intercept whoever it was. As Grace had predicted, it was Carl.

Rafa gave him a cheerful wave. "Hi. Grace and I were just checking for booby traps. Want to help me inspect the dressing rooms while Grace finishes up backstage?"

Carl obediently followed him to the dressing rooms, greeting Grace casually as they passed her. She was crouched down with her back turned, pretending to examine a trap door. Rafa let Carl inspect the dressing rooms while he watched. The assistant didn't seem to suspect anything, and they found nothing amiss.

By the time they returned, Grace was climbing down from the booth, all zipped up and with no evidence that she'd had multiple orgasms fifteen minutes ago other than slightly rumpled hair and an aura of satisfaction. When Carl went into the audience and had his back turned, she threw Rafa a wink and a whisper of, "Just erased the tape."

"Too bad, I was hoping to save it for a rainy day," Rafa whispered back with a grin.

The rest of the cast, crew, and musicians began to trickle in.

Melissa paused in the door, one hand flung out dramatically. "Wait! Is that sewer vermin here? That hideous rabid rat?"

Ruth did indeed have Tycho perched on her shoulder. Defensively, she said, "He's not rabid, and I'm sure he's never been any closer to a sewer than you have. Anyway, he won't leave my shoulder."

Melissa edged in, glaring at Ruth and Tycho every step of the way. "It better not."

"He won't," Ruth assured her. "He's obviously well-trained."

I bet he is, thought Rafa.

Grace apparently had the exact same thought. From across the room, they traded glances.

Paris swept in, carrying a picnic basket and a large tray covered in tin foil. "Gather round! I come bearing cupcakes!"

Lubomir checked his watch. "We've still got fifteen minutes. Cupcake break, everyone!"

"Can we get Mars rock seven onstage?" Grace called. "And a sheet of plastic to protect it?"

Several stagehands laid a large, flat Mars rock onstage and covered it with a clear plastic drop cloth. At Grace's instructions, they also laid out rows of odd-looking chairs.

"Space shuttle seats," she explained to Rafa.

Everyone settled into the seats. With great ceremony, Paris laid out paper plates, plastic silverware, and finally a thermos and a bundled-up cloth napkin, which she unwrapped to reveal a little china teacup with a matching saucer. "For your chamomile tea, Ruth."

The scientist smiled, her cheeks flushing pink. "You're so sweet."

"Everyone else fends for themselves for drinks," Paris went on.

She gave Carl a meaningful glance. With a small sigh and a mutter under his breath of "coffee with cream, coffee with sugar and cream, coffee with neither," he went out.

"And now! The grand unveiling!" With a dramatic flourish, Paris lifted the tin foil. A series of excited gasps and murmurs arose. Rafa caught Paris's eye across the cupcakes and grinned at her. She winked back.

He had to admit, she had outdone herself. The cupcakes looked like they'd been made by a professional baker. More importantly, they looked absolutely delicious.

"AIEEEEE!"

A shriek split the ear, and nearly split Rafa's eardrums. It was Melissa. Again. Tycho had leaped off Ruth's shoulder and was making a beeline for the cupcakes.

Ruth snatched him away just in time. "I'm so sorry, Melissa. I'll put him in his cage until the cupcakes are gone. I guess he's got a sweet tooth."

As she went to pop him into a little carrying cage, Rafa asked Paris,

"Is there vanilla in any of the cupcakes?"

"It's in all of them, actually. Not enough to taste, except for the vanilla cupcakes there." Paris indicated a few white-frosted cupcakes. "But adding a little vanilla to the batter just makes it taste better. Why? You're not allergic, are you?"

Rafa gave her his most innocent smile. "Just wondering if that was what smelled so good."

He and Grace again exchanged glances. He'd double-check with the bottle of vanilla extract later, in case the little white rat really did just have a sweet tooth, but he was already convinced that his theory was right: Tycho had been trained.

"What are they all?" a stagehand asked.

"Hang on. Let's wait till everyone's here." But Paris had apparently forgotten or didn't care about Carl, because as soon as Ruth returned to her place at the Mars rock table, she launched into her cupcake explanation. "Those luscious, gooey, chocolately ones are lava cupcakes. Just for you, Ruth! Eat one quick, while it's still warm from the oven."

"Warm from the oven," Ruth echoed. "Just for me?"

With a smile, Paris put one on a plate and slid it over to her, along with a knife and fork. "I'd cut it instead of just biting into it, if I was you."

Ruth sliced into the cupcake. Hot fudge oozed out, sending up tiny wisps of steam in the cool theatre. She took a bite, and a positively orgasmic expression came over her face. Her voice a bit muffled, she murmured, "Incredible."

Paris watched Ruth eat, looking as pleased as Rafa had ever seen her, until Brady nudged her. "What are the rest of them?"

"Right!" Paris seemed to visibly force her attention from Ruth to the cupcakes. "The ones with a chunk of Snickers bar on top are Snickers cupcakes: chocolate cake with caramel and peanuts. The chocolate cupcakes with just chocolate frosting on top are regular chocolate, the plain white cupcakes are vanilla, and the white ones with sprinkles are birthday cake."

She looked straight at Rafa, grinning, as she went on, "And I made some unusual cupcakes for Grace. The pink ones with crushed peppermint candy on top are peppermint stick, the light brown ones with white frosting are root beer float, and the light brown ones with a caramel drizzle are caramel-bacon."

Lubomir put down the caramel-drizzled cupcake he'd just picked up and took a Snickers cupcake instead. Grace helped herself to his unwanted bacon cupcake.

"And the pink ones with the rose petal on top are rose-flavored," Paris concluded.

"Your favorite, Rafa," said Grace, putting a rose-flavored cupcake on his plate.

She undoubtedly wouldn't mind knowing he'd fantasized about making love to her on a bed of rose petals, but he could hardly explain that in public as the reason for her misunderstanding. Valiantly, he took a bite. It tasted like soap.

"Delicious," he said. Out of the corner of his eye, he could see Paris trying not to burst out laughing.

Her voice quivering slightly, she said, "I bought rose water just for you, Rafa."

"You're a true friend," he said, then broke the cupcake in half. "You have to try this, Grace."

She ate her half with every appearance of sincere enjoyment. "Thanks, Rafa. Paris, these are amazing."

"Thanks," Paris said. She watched Ruth tip the thermos over her teacup. Only a few drops came out. "I have another thermos of tea in my dressing room. I'll go get it."

"You don't need—" Ruth began. But Paris was already out the door that led to the dressing rooms.

Rafa reached for a vanilla cupcake to forestall Grace handing him another frosted lump of baked perfume. But before he could pick it up, the other door opened. He glanced up, expecting to see Carl with everyone's coffee. And he did. But the person accompanying Carl was about the last one Rafa expected—or wanted—to see at the theatre.

It was his teammate Nick. His mate Raluca stood beside him, with Manuel lurking behind them and looking around, wide-eyed.

"I do hope we aren't intruding," Raluca said to the room at large. "Carl said you were on a break."

"They said they're Rafa's friends," Carl explained to Grace. "I told them it was fine to come in and say hi. It is, right?"

"*Are* they friends of yours?" Grace asked Rafa softly.

With no other alternative, he admitted, "Yes."

"Sure, it's fine," Grace told them. "Come on in. Have a cupcake."

"Nick, what are you doing here?" Rafa tried to speak for Nick's ears only, but Grace was right next to him. He did his best not to look at her.

Nick shrugged. "We picked up Manuel at the airport, and the theatre's on the way to our apartment. I pointed it out and mentioned you were working here, and he wanted to stop by and—"

"Rafa!" Manuel flung his long arms around Rafa's chest. "It's so great to see you! You know, I don't think I ever thanked you for what you did for me, but you changed my life. So thank you. I wouldn't be where I am now without you."

"You're welcome." Rafa tried to return the hug with the warmth he actually felt for the kid, but nine-tenths of his mind was occupied with the disaster that would ensue if Nick spotted how Rafa looked at Grace or how she looked at him, realized that they were mates, and decided to haze her on the spot. He had to get them all out of there as quickly as possible. And without giving them any reason to notice Grace.

So rather than introducing them to her or anyone, Rafa said, "Great to see you too, Manuel. Want to go outside and catch up?"

"Sure!" Manuel let Rafa lead him one step away, then stopped. "Wait, are you allowed to leave the theatre? Nick said you're bodyguarding the leading lady."

Before Rafa could reply, Nick glanced around the theatre and casually asked a question that struck him like a bullet: "Speaking of your ex-wife, where is she?"

CHAPTER TEN

Grace

"Your ex-wife."

The words struck Grace to the heart.

She stared at Rafa, hoping against hope that she'd somehow misheard or misunderstood. But the shock, horror, and guilt written all over his face told her everything she needed to know.

The words flew out of her mouth as fast as she could think them: "Ex-wife? Ex-*wife?* You and Paris used to be *married?!* You said you'd never been romantically involved!"

"We weren't!" Rafa exclaimed. "Yes, we did used to be married, but only—"

Paris's clear voice cut through his deep one; she'd returned from the dressing room and was standing with a thermos dangling from her hand. "Rafa, you didn't tell her?"

"I was going to—I was waiting for the right moment—" he protested.

"The *right moment* would have been before we had sex!" Grace shouted.

"You had sex with the bodyguard?" Brady asked, at the same moment that Paris said accusingly to Rafa, "You had sex with Grace and you didn't tell her?"

"Yeah, but—" Rafa began.

"How could you?" said the silver-haired woman.

"What the hell, man!" exclaimed Rafa's friend Nick.

Rafa turned to Grace. He looked like he'd been stabbed in the heart, but that didn't make her feel any better. She worked with actors. A good actor could make himself show any emotion he liked. Her ex-boyfriend Dean had been a very good actor.

"I'm so, so sorry." Rafa sounded sincere. But then, he would. "I should have told you right away. But it's not what you think. We were only married for—"

Liar, Grace thought, the storm in her mind too loud to hear the rest of what he was saying. *Cheater. Too good to be true.*

Anger and sadness fought within her, and sadness won. She burst into tears.

Yesterday, she would have thought that crying in front of everyone and on the job would be her worst nightmare come true. But now she knew what her real worst nightmare was. It was meeting a man who she'd dared to dream might be *her* man. Her one-and-only, forever. And then discovering that he was just the pretense of a good guy, not the real thing; an actor playing a role, as fake as the Mars rocks made of painted canvas stretched over a wooden frame.

After a few minutes, she became vaguely aware of assorted actors and stagehands and musicians trying to comfort her, and also of Rafa and Nick shouting at each other.

"You never fucking told me not to mention that Paris was your ex!" Nick yelled.

"She's *not* my ex, that's the thing!" Rafa's deep voice seemed to shake the rafters.

"How the hell is she not your ex when you were fucking *married?!"* Nick retorted.

"Hey! Can you two have this discussion outside?" Lubomir broke in. "We have work to do in here."

"I can't leave. I'm guarding everyone," Rafa protested.

The silver-haired woman cleared her throat. "Nick, Manuel, let's go. We can sort this out at some better time and place."

Nick's green eyes flashed angrily, but he acquiesced. "Fine. Me and Manuel can go hunting, like we planned."

Manuel dragged his feet as Nick and the silver-haired woman started to hustle him out the door. "Could we come back later?"

"Yeah, sure," Nick threw out, his words clearly aimed more at Rafa than at the college kid. "We'll come back when things are less fucked up, if they're ever less fucked up."

When the door closed behind them, a heavy silence fell across the theatre. Grace dragged her arm across her eyes, willing herself to stop crying. Her sleeve came back soaking wet.

"Grace, why don't you take a break?" Lubomir suggested. "As long as you like. Carl can run things for a while."

"Absolutely," said Carl.

Rafa looked grateful for the suggestion. To Grace, he said, "Let's go outside and talk. I can explain—"

"NO!" Grace was startled by her own voice, both by how loud it was and by its sheer rage. "You lied to me. I don't want to talk to you. I don't even want to *see* you. If you respect me at all, you'll go away. Without arguing. NOW."

She stared at Rafa, willing him to leave. But she was wearily certain that he wouldn't. Sure, he'd given lip service to respecting women's choices. But he was a cheater and liar, just like Dean. And just like Dean, he'd ignore what she'd said and say she didn't understand and let me just explain and give me one more chance and—

"All right," Rafa said. "I'm going outside to guard the theatre, but I'll call one of my teammates to take over for me. I'll leave as soon as they get here. If you do decide you want to talk, they all have my number. I hope you do. But I know I screwed up. And I'm not going to be one of those assholes who doesn't take no for an answer."

To Grace's shock, he turned around and walked out.

The silence that fell after he was gone felt different from the last one. That one had felt as if it was silent because she was locked up alone and underground. This one felt as if it was silent because she was alone in a room where anyone might walk in and say something—maybe someone she wanted to see, saying something she wanted to hear.

"I don't know if you want to hear anything from me," Paris said quietly. "I realize that I'm the ex-wife..."

Grace sniffed hard and said, "I heard what you said to him. You thought he'd told me already. I'm not mad at *you*."

"In that case..." Oddly, Paris wasn't looking at Grace. For some reason, she was watching Ruth as she spoke. "I'm not saying you shouldn't be mad at Rafa. He *should* have told you we used to be married. But it actually is true that we were never romantically involved."

“Why would you get married if you weren’t?” Grace asked, unsure if she even believed Paris.

“Well… If there was something you wanted to cover up… Something you didn’t want people to know… Something *I* didn’t want people to know…” Paris took a deep breath and seemed to brace herself. Raising her voice, she announced to the entire theatre. “Something like not being into guys.”

Grace was startled. It was so completely different from anything she’d expected Paris to say. And then, thinking back to so many little moments during rehearsals, she wasn’t surprised at all. More than that, she knew in her heart that Paris was telling the truth.

Paris looked straight at Ruth as she said, “I like women. I’ve only ever liked women. And right now, I like one specific woman… One beautiful, brilliant woman who likes math and Mars and chocolate fudge cupcakes, and has the cutest rescue pet ever.”

“Oh my God,” Ruth blurted out. “I thought it was just me. I wasn’t going to say anything about the huge crush I had on you, when you were probably straight or not into scientists or just not into me—”

“Oh, I am *so* into you, Ruth,” Paris broke in.

The women practically fell into each other’s arms. Paris reached up and tugged the pins out of Ruth’s hair, making it fall down her back. It was as long as Paris’s own.

They didn’t stop kissing until Lubomir cleared his throat. “Congratulations!”

At that, they broke apart, both looking radiant. And also slightly guilty.

“I hate to interrupt you lovebirds,” Lubomir went on, “But we’re incredibly late for the rehearsal. So here’s my acting note for you for the next scene, Paris: pretend that Brady is Ruth.”

“That’s why I didn’t come out till now,” Paris admitted. “I was afraid audiences wouldn’t accept me playing romantic leads with men if they knew.”

“It’s acting, Paris,” Brady pointed out. “I don’t actually want to have sex with you either.”

Angry mutters arose from a violinist, an actress, and a stagehand. “She’d be the first woman you didn’t!”

“We need to rehearse now,” Lubomir said.

Everyone kept on talking. Automatically, Grace raised her voice so it would echo across the theatre: "PLACES PLEASE! Everyone, please take your places!"

Everyone stopped talking and hurried to their places. Grace sat down with her laptop, put on her headset, and lit the stage.

"Stand by to bring on the crashed spaceship," she began. "Stand by for the "Mars at night" backdrop. Stand by..."

As she continued speaking, she realized that for the last few minutes, she'd gotten so caught up in her work and in the reveal of Paris and Ruth's secret crush, she'd forgotten her own heartbreak. Instantly, the memory of Rafa being unmasked as a liar returned, hitting her like a kick in the stomach.

But as her voice flowed on and her fingers tapped the keys, she followed that thought. It was true that he hadn't told her something that he should have. But he'd apparently been honest about the most important thing: he and Paris hadn't been in love. From what Paris had said, it sounded like their marriage had been a sham to protect her and her career.

And even if there had been more to it than that, it was obvious that it was over now. Sure, they liked each other. As friends. She'd seen how Paris looked at Rafa, and how she looked at Ruth. More importantly, she'd seen how Rafa looked at Paris, and how he looked at her.

She thought again about Paris and Ruth. Their romance had been going on right under her nose, and Grace had never noticed—she'd been too wrapped up in her own romance. But everything wasn't about her. Other people had their own lives, their own secrets, and their own reasons for doing things. Just because Grace had been burned by a charming cheater once didn't mean that all charming men were cheaters.

Rafa must have had his reasons for keeping his secret. Maybe they had nothing to do with being a liar or a cheater or trying to trick her, any more than Paris's secret made her a liar or a cheater or trying to trick Ruth.

He should have told her. But she could guess why he hadn't. If one of her exes had been working on the show with her—if, say, Lubomir was her ex-husband—she'd have been nervous about telling Rafa too.

Besides, he *had* respected her. She'd told him to leave, and he'd left—but he'd made sure she was protected first.

Maybe he wasn't too good to be true, after all.

As soon as the rehearsal was over, she'd call him up, listen to what he had to say, and only then make up her mind.

With that decision, a weight seemed to lift from Grace's chest.

And a second later, it came crashing down again. She'd refused to listen to his explanation, yelled at him, called him a liar, and kicked him out of the theatre.

Sure, she'd give him another chance. But would *he* give *her* another chance?

CHAPTER ELEVEN

Rafa

Rafa stood outside the theatre with half a rose-flavored cupcake in his hand and his heart in shattered pieces in his chest.

Go back inside, roared his lion. *Chase down your mate and* make *her listen.*

No, replied Rafa for what felt like the millionth time. *She's been hurt before by a man who chased her down and tried to* make *her listen. I won't do that to her.*

His lion wasn't listening. He roared again, louder and more frantically than ever. *Pursue her! Explain it to her! Don't let her get away!*

The roar was silent and inside his head, but it still made Rafa's ears ring. But it only strengthened his resolve to give his mate space to make her own decisions. Having his lion demand his attention and refuse to listen to what he was saying gave him just the smallest taste of what it would feel like to Grace if he strode back in and demanded that she hear him out, like it or not.

I have to watch for danger, Rafa said. *I can't if you keep roaring at me. I need to protect my mate, remember?*

With a final muttered growl of *Chase her, chase her,* his lion subsided.

Rafa's head ached. His chest hurt like he'd been stabbed in the heart. He wished an assassin would show up. A shoot-out would make a wonderful break from having to stand there and think about how he'd ruined his own life.

Instead, Destiny's car pulled up. It wasn't the distraction he'd hoped for, but it would do. He'd called her on the basis that Grace would probably prefer a woman, Fiona was either at the opera or already busy investigating *My Fair Lady*, and Catalina preferred to work in a team with her mate and Shane was the single most intimidating member of Protection, Inc.

Destiny walked up, her many braids whipping around her face in the chilly winter wind. "Brr. What's up, Rafa?"

He was beyond tempted to leave out the reason why his client had kicked his ass to the curb. But even apart from the likelihood of Destiny hearing the story straight from the horse's mouth once the rehearsal ended, Rafa was done with lying. Even lies of omission, like that one. Even little white lies, like the bed full of identical twins. One lie of omission, another of misdirection, a little white lie or two, and here he was, shivering outside with an icy cold void where his heart used to be instead of warm inside with his beautiful mate.

"I screwed up, Destiny," he admitted. And he told her the entire story.

When he finished, she looked at him with both frustration and sympathy. "Good Lord, Rafa. You said you were 'never romantically involved' with your *ex-wife?* Yeah, I believe you that you weren't, but you can't say that when you haven't even mentioned that you *have* an ex-wife!"

"I know," he said glumly. "Don't rub it in, okay? I *know.* Hey, did you come from the office? Was anyone else there?"

Destiny raised her eyebrows. "Why, are you planning to avoid the team for the rest of your life?"

"Just for the rest of today," he admitted. "Come on, Destiny. Is it safe for me to go back?"

"Yeah, no one's around. Hey." She unexpectedly threw her arm around his shoulders, standing on tiptoe to do it. "It'll be all right. She's your mate. Everyone says mates have an infinite ability to work things out."

"I hope so." He didn't believe it for a second.

Destiny smacked him across the back of the head.

"Ow! What was that for?"

"For being an idiot," she said cheerfully. "And sounding like Eeyore just now. Go on, slink on back to the office. Then go home. And don't try to drown your sorrows. I bet your mate asks me for your phone number and calls you as soon as she's done with work, and you don't want to be dead drunk when you pick up the phone."

The thought of drowning his sorrows had indeed crossed his mind, and he was grateful to Destiny for warning him. But he was hardly going to say so. "I weigh over two hundred pounds. And I'm a shifter. It'd take enough whiskey to fill a swimming pool to get *me* dead drunk."

Destiny chuckled. Then she glanced down at his hand. "Hey, what's that pink thing you're holding?"

"Believe it or not, it's half a rose-flavored cupcake." Rafa tossed it to her. She caught it automatically. "Enjoy. Maybe."

Her laugh echoed in his ears as he walked away.

The drive back to the Protection, Inc. offices felt like it took forever, though it was only half an hour or so. He hoped nobody had showed up in the time between when Destiny had left and he'd arrived. He'd vowed to stop lying, and the last thing he wanted was to have to repeat the story of what a thoughtless idiot he'd been and how he'd gotten his mate so pissed off that she never wanted to see him again. In fact, if he saw anyone's cars in the underground parking garage, he'd turn around and go home.

There were no cars in the garage. Relieved, he parked and took the elevator up to the lobby. He'd just return his gun to the weapons room and go home.

Rafa stepped into the lobby, and was confronted with his entire team. Their mates too.

He froze in the doorway, too shocked and horrified to move, let alone speak. Then he took a second look. It wasn't *quite* the entire team. Fiona wasn't there; he supposed she was still at the opera. Neither, of course, was Destiny. But everyone else was, including Nick and Raluca.

In other words, all the mated pairs were there. They stood or sat next to each other, shoulder to shoulder or with their hands clasped or toying with each other's hair. Just what he needed, a visual representation of the love he'd thrown away.

"You ambushed me," Rafa said indignantly. "Where are your cars?"

"Parked around the block," said Shane. "Destiny said you'd probably turn around and leave if you saw them."

"You got that right." Glumly, Rafa went to the sofa and sat down.

"Fine. Lay it on me. Tell me what an idiot I was."

There was a brief silence, and then Hal said in his rumbling voice, "Buddy, you got the wrong end of the stick. Destiny didn't call us in to chew you out. She called us in to cheer you up."

Rafa blinked. "She did?"

Everyone nodded.

"But she told you what *I* did?" Rafa felt like he'd gotten drunk after all.

"She told us everything," Lucas said in his lightly accented voice. "The entire story. She set up a group call so we'd all hear at the same time. That's how we were able to get here so quickly."

Rafa looked at Nick. "*You* came to cheer me up?"

"Yeah, I did." Nick shrugged. "Hey, I'm the one who fucked it up for you with my big mouth, the least I could do was come and say I'm sorry."

"You didn't fuck it up for me," Rafa muttered. "I did that all by myself."

"Well, we've all been there," Hal said. "Every single one of us. That's why Destiny called us, so we could tell you that this isn't the end of everything."

"None of you ever screwed up like I did," Rafa said. "I didn't tell my mate I'd been *married.*"

Lucas twisted the golden wedding ring on his finger. "I didn't tell my mate I was about to get engaged in an arranged marriage to a woman I didn't love."

Journey squeezed his hand. "To be fair, we'd only just met. If we'd gotten ten more minutes alone, you would have."

Lucas didn't argue.

Mine was worse, Rafa thought. Lucas had delayed revealing crucial information by accident, not on purpose.

Very quietly, Shane said, "I didn't tell my mate I used to be an assassin."

Catalina jumped in. "You mean, that you'd been *forced* to be an assassin! That doesn't count."

Mine is still worse, Rafa thought. He knew that though Shane had worried that Catalina would reject him if she knew about his past, she had never once blamed him for it.

Hal's deep voice filled the room. "I drove a car with my mate in the passenger seat for three hours without telling her I'd been shot, quietly bleeding beneath my overcoat, until I nearly got us both killed by passing out at the wheel."

"Okay, that's actually worse than what I did," Rafa admitted.

"I can top that," said Nick. "I made my mate eat a bacon-wrapped hot dog from a place that's famous for having a giant bacon-wrapped hot dog on the roof and serving the worst fucking bacon-wrapped hot dogs in all of creation."

Rafa would not have imagined that he could ever laugh again after his mate rejected him. But that did it. And once he'd laughed, he was able to see the point his team had been making. "Okay. You win. If Raluca forgave you for Big Bacon, maybe Grace will forgive me for not telling her about Paris."

"Ellie was furious with me over not telling her I'd been shot," Hal said. "She ripped me a new one. And it was well-deserved. But she forgave me too."

"Only because you never did it again," Ellie remarked.

"I'm not lying to Grace again," Rafa said. "If she calls me, I'm telling her about shifters first thing. Well, maybe not over the phone. I feel like that'll go better if I have a chance to demonstrate."

"Yeah, definitely wait till you can demonstrate," said Ellie. "When Hal told me I thought he was delirious."

"Do not despair," said Raluca. "Mates are not so easy to lose. Nick and I had moments when we were enraged with each other. I almost flung him from a speeding car. And yet here we are."

"I got so mad at her, I made her sit in a car with me listening to the worst music on the fucking planet. Which is why she nearly tossed me out of it." Nick traced one of her silver dragonmarks with a finger. "But here we are."

Hope bloomed in Rafa's heart. Maybe they were right. "Hey… If it does work out, will you all promise not to haze her? The joke's getting old."

"You can introduce your mate to me without fear," Raluca assured him.

"You're not the one I'm worried about." Rafa looked at Nick. "What about you?"

"Bring her in," Nick said with a shrug. "I won't bite."

"Hal?"

Hal evaded Rafa's gaze. "No promises. I'll play it by ear."

Ellie stared at her mate. "What? But you never get in on the hazing."

"Actually…" Catalina began, then cut herself off. "Oops."

Ellie's jaw dropped. "What? Hal hazed you? You never told me—neither of you ever told me!"

A three-way flurry of explanations and indignant questioning broke out. Rafa left them to it. "Shane?"

Shane's ice-blue eyes didn't blink. "I'm with Hal. No promises. I'll play it by ear."

"Oh, come on, guys!" Rafa burst out. "This is ridiculous. How am I supposed to introduce you to my mate when I know for a fact that you're going to try to scare her off?"

A sudden silence fell. As Rafa replayed his words in his mind, he realized that his team's mission had succeeded. The only reason he was worrying about his team hazing his mate was that he now thought he *would* introduce her to them.

We have not *lost our mate forever,* his lion rumbled. *Soon we will be together again.*

"You win," Rafa said. "Thanks for coming out. I'm going home now. I have to wait for a phone call."

CHAPTER TWELVE

Grace

The rest of the rehearsal felt like it lasted an eternity. Even when it ended, Grace still had to endure watching Paris and Ruth stroll out together, Paris carrying her empty cupcake tray and Ruth her empty rat cage, with their free hands clasped tight. Tycho rode on Ruth's shoulder. They looked so happy and in love, and walked so close together that Ruth's brown hair, which she'd never pinned back up, mingled with Paris's blonde locks.

When everyone had finally left, Grace forced herself to her feet. Time to meet the replacement bodyguard and ask for Rafa's phone number.

Time to find out if she'd thrown away her own best chance at love.

The night was dark and cold, and a bitter wind struck through her clothes the instant she opened the theatre door. A curvy black woman stood outside, her attitude relaxed but watchful. Just like Rafa.

That thought made Grace feel like she'd been stabbed in the heart with a sliver of glass.

The woman turned around. "Grace?"

"Yes."

"I'm Rafa's replacement."

That one little word enlarged the splinter of glass in Grace's heart to a shard, its edges cruelly sharp and cutting.

"He had to go home sick," the woman bodyguard said. "I mean, he didn't say that, but I assume that's why he called me in. He looked terrible. You know, Rafa's a former Navy SEAL, and they're awfully stoic.

And macho. I remember once we got in a throwdown with a gang, and he got his arm slashed open. We came back to our office, and he was bleeding all over the floor. We have a paramedic on staff, and she sewed up his arm. He never flinched. Cracked jokes the entire time. But today, I could see he was hurting."

The bodyguard shook her head, looking concerned. "Man, I hope he's all right. He was obviously in pain. And for him to show it at all, it must've been bad. I've never seen that kind of suffering in a man's eyes before."

Forget being stabbed. Grace felt like her heart had been run through a wood chipper. Which was apparently exactly what she'd done to Rafa.

The woman studied her face. And then, bizarrely, she smiled and said cheerfully, "But I'm sure he'll be fine. He's a tough guy. Shall I walk you to your car?"

Grace edged a step back. No sane person's mood changed *that* fast. "No, thanks. I, uh, I'm not leaving yet. I still have work to do. Can I have Rafa's phone number, though? I want to tell him to get well soon."

The woman passed her a piece of paper. "Here you go. Give him my best."

"Absolutely," Grace said, and bolted back into the theatre. What a weird woman! She'd have expected a bodyguard—especially a bodyguard from Rafa's agency—to be more professional.

Once she was backstage, she sank down on the nearest Mars rock, her heart sledgehammering against her ribcage. The slip of paper with Rafa's number felt like it was burning through her palm. She'd never been more afraid of anything than she was afraid of calling him. What if he hated her? What if he rejected her? What if he couldn't forgive her?

"Huh," Grace muttered aloud. "Whatever happened to 'what if he really is a charming cheater?'"

But speaking those words aloud destroyed the last of their power. She was suddenly certain that he wasn't. Sure, some people were good actors. But her heart told her that Rafa was exactly what he seemed to be: a good man.

She took a deep breath and dialed the number.

"Rafa?"

"Grace!" Just hearing his voice made her feel warm inside. "I'm so glad you called. Can we talk in person?"

"Yes." She was relieved that she didn't have to have an intense conversation over the phone, and also that he didn't sound either angry with her or as devastated as his weird co-worker had made out. "I'm still at the theatre. Everyone else is gone. Sorry to make you leave and then come back—"

"I'll be right over." The phone went dead.

Grace walked around the theatre while she waited for him to arrive, putting props back in place and checking for booby traps. She'd been so distracted that last rehearsal, they'd all been incredibly lucky that the theatre villain hadn't chosen to strike that day. Or maybe Rafa had scared him off.

When she went to inspect the dressing rooms, she found a paper plate wrapped in tin foil and a post-it note reading, "GRACE - Cupcakes for you. Enjoy. I hope you get to share them. Love, Paris."

Grace lifted the tin foil. Paris had set aside one each of the caramel-bacon, root beer float, rose, and Snickers cupcakes. How thoughtful! Grace could certainly use a sugar rush right about now.

She took them backstage and put them on a convenient Mars rock. Just then, the door opened.

Rafa stood in the doorway with a bunch of red roses. At the sight of him, all of Grace's complicated feelings returned in a rush. She wanted to run to him and kiss him. She wanted to yell at him for throwing a monkey wrench into their relationship. She wanted to apologize for yelling at him. She wanted him to tell her everything would be all right.

Grace held out the cupcakes. "Rose cupcake?"

Rafa held out the bouquet. "Actual roses?"

"Trade you," Grace said.

She took the red roses, and he took a pink cupcake.

"No. Wait." Rafa began to speak very quickly. "First thing. I want you to know that I've sworn that I will never lie to you again. Not a lie of omission, not a lie to make you feel better, not a little white lie, not even a tiny lie of politeness like eating food I don't like because it's rude not to take what you've offered me."

He replaced the cupcake on the plate.

Grace blinked at the rush of words, not to mention the return of the cupcake. "So… You don't actually like rose cupcakes?"

"I don't," Rafa said promptly. "They taste like soap. Do you seriously enjoy them?"

"I do! They're so delicate and perfume-y. Like eating flowers."

"Yecch. Okay, second thing. Before I say anything else, I want you to know that there's something else I didn't tell you. It isn't anything bad, but I was worried that you wouldn't understand. Also, it's kind of, um, a lot to take in. But I'm going to tell you tonight. Right after I tell you what was up with me and Paris. Or before, I guess. Up to you."

He'd been talking very fast, then stopped as suddenly as if someone had put their hand over his mouth.

"Whoa, cowboy." Grace marched up and grabbed his arm. The muscle was solid under her palm. She loved how strong he was. But he let her steer him to a Mars rock and sit him down on it.

"You don't need to tell me all your secrets in the next ten seconds," she informed him. "First, have a cupcake that you actually want. Unless you hate cupcakes in general. But you sound like you drank about a gallon of coffee and didn't eat anything all day."

"Yeah, I guess I did forget to eat," he admitted. "And I did drink a lot of coffee. It was that or drink a lot of whiskey, which one of my teammates warned me off doing."

"Smart guy."

"Smart girl," Rafa corrected her. "But thanks. I'll try the Snickers. I'm not much for unusual."

"More for me."

She stuck the actual roses in a prop beaker from a lab scene and helped herself to his rejected rose cupcake. Then they sat together on the Mars rock and ate their cupcakes. It felt as companionable as if they were having a picnic. Strange. They still hadn't hashed out their horrendous fight earlier, and he'd just told her he had *another* secret. Grace should have felt incredibly on edge. Instead, she felt peaceful. And though Rafa had been practically vibrating with tension when he'd come in, he relaxed as he ate.

"Try the root beer float," she suggested. "It's really not that weird."

"Hmm." He looked doubtful, and broke off a small piece to try. "Oh, hey, yeah, you're right. That's actually good."

Grace ate the caramel-bacon cupcake without offering him any. She knew perfectly well how weird that one was, even though it was also pure salty-sweet deliciousness.

"Something you should know," she said as Rafa finished his root beer float cupcake. "Right after you left, Paris came out to the entire theatre. She and Ruth are madly in love."

"No way!" His face lit up with genuine delight. "Oh, that's great. I'm so happy for her. That was never a secret she wanted to keep. She just felt like she had to."

"Well, the cat's out of the bag now. Sorry, I should have told you as soon as you walked in. I assume you only married her so everyone would think she was straight?"

Rafa ran his fingers through his midnight hair. "Not exactly. You know… I think that story is actually going to make more sense if I tell you something else first."

"Your other secret?"

"Yeah." He took a deep breath. "I know this is going to sound weird…"

"I like weird," Grace pointed out. "I *am* weird."

"You're not *weird.*" He sounded indignant on her behalf. "You're different. Quirky. Original."

"Those are all just nice ways of saying weird. So go on. Tell me your weird secret."

He seemed to brace himself before he spoke. "You know how every culture has myths about shapeshifters?"

"Oh, sure. There's a family legend on my mom's side that some of our ancestors could turn into tigers."

"There is?!" Rafa sounded much more shocked than she'd expected him to be, especially since he was the one who had brought up shapeshifters.

"Really. In fact…" Grace hesitated, but only from habit. Was he surprised because his secret was the same as hers? How funny and ironic if it was! "Supposedly I have a cousin who's a were-tiger. It's this big family secret, though I don't really get why. I've never been able to figure out if it's a family in-joke to pretend it's true or if some people really believe it. I assume she's the female version of 'Florida Man Claims To Be Tiger, Moves Into Zoo.' She lives in Santa Martina and I'd never been here till I moved last year, so I've never met her. I sure wasn't about to look her up. So, same for you? Freaky family legends that your great-grandma sprouted fur every full moon?"

Rafa's dark eyes had grown wider and wider as she spoke. At that, he began to laugh. When he spoke, there was a quiver in his voice, as if he might start cracking up again at any second. "Yeah. There are. But it's not just on a full moon, it's not just my great-grandma, and it's not tigers. It's lions."

"No wonder you've got a mane," she teased, giving his hair a tug.

"That's right. And also… hang on, this is the part I need to show you…" He pulled off his shirt, then his shoes.

Puzzled, Grace watched as he unzipped his jeans. "You have a birthmark shaped like a lion's paw?"

"Nope." He pulled off his jeans and boxers, and stood nude before her. But she didn't have time to enjoy looking at his body, because what he said next captured her attention. "I'm going to show you something much more weird and amazing than that. You see, I think your family legend might not be just a legend. Because mine isn't."

With that, Rafa vanished and a lion appeared.

Grace dropped her cupcake plate. "Oh my God!"

The lion shook his head, sending his mane flying. Strands of hair brushed against her bare hands. She could feel their rough texture and smell the lion's pleasant scent of clean fur. The lion's breath was warm on her face, and he regarded her calmly with his huge dark eyes.

They were Rafa's eyes: that soft, deep, amber-touched brown.

Her shock gave way to wonder. So the legends were real. At least, Rafa's was real. She'd seen plenty of illusion—it was the business of theatre—but this lion was no trick like the painted "Mars rocks" or overhead lights made to look like stars. It was a living, breathing beast that she could touch and smell.

The lion nuzzled her. She stroked his velvety fur. A deep rumble filled her ears, and the lion's body vibrated against her hands. He was purring.

Grace petted him for a while, lost in amazement at his transformation and the delight of getting to pet the world's biggest and best cat. She buried her hands in his mane and gave it a little tug. He purred louder.

"Can you turn back?" she asked.

In the next instant, her hands were full of Rafa's silky hair.

"That's incredible," she breathed, letting it slide through her fingers like rain.

"You see why I was nervous about telling you." He began to dress again. "I was afraid you'd think I was crazy if I told you, and I was afraid I'd scare you if I just suddenly shifted."

"Shifted," Grace repeated. "Amazing! Were you born like that, or bitten by a were-lion?"

"Born like that. My family's always been lion shifters. That's what I started to say when I was talking about the women in my family. It's not just that they're strong. It's that in the wild, it's the lionesses who hunt."

"And the lions laze around and eat the meat," she teased. "No wonder you've got such great hair! It's your duty to keep your mane perfect for the ladies."

Rafa's eyebrows rose. "Were you joking? That's actually true. Lion shifters believe that a lion's mane shows his masculinity. That goes for my hair as a man, too. It damn near killed me to get a buzz cut when I joined the Navy. Honestly half the reason I went for SEALs was because Special Forces don't have to cut their hair short."

"Like the way the size of your hands is supposed to represent the size of your dick?"

"Not quite, or my hair would be down to my ass." Rafa ducked as Grace threw a playful punch at his arm. More seriously, he said, "Your mane shows your vitality and masculine energy, and you keep it perfectly groomed to demonstrate that you're keeping yourself in good shape for the ladies."

"Lots of masculine energy there. Not to mention perfect grooming," Grace remarked, stroking his hair. Then she remembered the other thing he'd said. "Wait a second. You said my family legend might not be a legend. Do you think my cousin really can turn into a tiger?"

"Maybe. It'd be unusual if she's the only one in the family who can, but that happens sometimes. If shifters only marry non-shifters for a long time, sometimes the ability dies out. She might be a throwback—the first person in generations who can shift. I know someone like that. She's a tiger shifter too, actually. In fact—" He broke off. "What's your cousin's name?"

"Destiny Ford."

Rafa burst out laughing. "She's on my team! Didn't you recognize her? She's the one who gave you my number."

"No way!" Grace shook her head in amazement, then laughed as well. "I never met her. I've seen some photos of her, but they were from years ago. She was in an Army uniform, with no makeup and her hair scraped back. It's hard to recognize people if you're not expecting to see them and they looked different in the pictures. If she hasn't seen any photos of me since I was a teenager, she was probably expecting a pink Mohawk."

Rafa blinked, clearly trying to visualize her with a pink Mohawk, then apparently gave up the attempt. "I still can't get over you two being related. Now that I know, you do have a similar body type. But just looking at your face, I can't see it."

"I take after Dad's side of the family," Grace explained. "His mother's Portuguese and his father's Chinese-American. Destiny and I are related through Mom, and that side of the family is African-American. Though maybe they're also part Indian or something. They don't have tigers in Africa, right?"

Rafa shook his head. "Tigers, no. Tiger *shifters*, sure. My family descended from Spanish conquistadores on one side and Aztec royalty on the other. If it went by what big cats lived where my family came from, I should either turn into a jaguar or an Iberian lynx. But no. It's lions all the way back."

"And Destiny's on your team? Do all of you turn into some sort of big cat?"

"No, but we all are shifters. Though now that you mention it, there *are* a lot of big cats. Fiona's a snow leopard, Catalina's a regular leopard, and Shane's a panther. Our boss, Hal, is a grizzly bear. Nick's a wolf. I didn't actually take Melissa's pants to a lab, I took them to the office and had Nick sniff them."

"Handy," Grace remarked.

"And Lucas is a dragon."

"He is not," she said instantly, sure he was pulling her leg.

"He is," Rafa replied, his eyes glinting with amusement. "I promised never to lie to you again, remember? Are you thinking there's no such thing as dragons? Because five minutes ago, you thought there was no such thing as shifters."

"How come no one's ever seen one?"

"I hate to say this, because it's going to sound even more implausible,"

Rafa said. "But dragons can turn invisible."

Grace opened her mouth to deny it, then closed it again. It was so much to take in. Rafa could turn into a lion. That weird woman he worked with was her black sheep cousin. Her family legend about were-tigers was true. Dragons were real.

"Okay," she said at last. "I just saw you turn into a lion, so I guess I can believe in bodyguards who turn into invisible dragons. But you said I should know about this before you told me about Paris. What does this have to do with her? Does she turn into a lion too?"

"She does have a good mane, doesn't she?" Rafa said with a grin. "Though not as pretty as yours. No, she's not a shifter. At least, not that I know of, and I know her well enough that I think I'd have figured it out."

"So you can't just… I don't know… magically detect each other?"

"Not really. Some types of shifters have identifying marks. And I think some types of shifters can sense each other. But most can't. Lions can't." He put his arm around Grace. She settled into his comforting warmth as he went on, "Shifters don't just have different animals we turn into, we have different customs and traditions, like non-shifters do. But there's some things we all have in common. We're stronger than non-shifters. We're harder to kill, and we heal much faster. But the most important thing is that we have the ability to recognize our mates."

"What's a mate?" Her voice cracked. She had a feeling that she already knew, and it made her nerves sing with hope that she was right, and fear that she was right about what mates were but that Rafa's mate wasn't her.

Rafa turned his head to look deep into her eyes. His voice deepened with heartfelt passion as he said, "Your mate is your true love. It's the person you're perfectly compatible with, the person you'll love forever, the person you can never fall out of love with. You're mine, Grace. I knew from the moment I first saw you. If you'll have me, I'm yours for as long as we both shall live."

"Oh, I'll have you!" The words flew out of her mouth before she could think about them. But she didn't have the slightest desire to take them back. She knew in her heart that he was the man for her, just as she was the woman for him.

Maybe it was her little bit of shifter ancestry that allowed her to recognize her mate. Or maybe it was just that when you meet your true love, you know.

He bent to kiss her. She kissed back with all the passion she'd had before, but also, for the first time, with trust and certainty.

"I love you," she said. "I nearly said it earlier. But I didn't trust myself. I thought it was too soon."

"I nearly said it earlier, too," Rafa confessed. "But I didn't trust in you. I thought you'd think I was coming on too strong."

"I probably would've. Well, you can come on as strong as you like now. I trust you." She shook her head, amazed at her own words. "That's a first. I hope you're okay with a mate who has trust issues."

"I'm not sure you're the one with the issues," Rafa replied. "Not everyone's trustworthy. There's nothing wrong with protecting yourself. And I'm sorry as hell that I wasn't honest with you right away."

"And I'm sorry I yelled at you and wouldn't let you explain," Grace said immediately. "I feel terrible about it. When Destiny gave me your number, she obviously had no idea what had happened—she thought you had to go home because you were sick—but—"

He looked baffled. "What? What did she say to you?"

"She described how awful you looked and how much you were suffering, and I knew it was because of me. I'd obviously really hurt you. I felt so guilty."

"She hazed you!" Rafa exclaimed. They were sitting so close that she heard the noise as he ground his teeth. "Goddammit. I thought I could get you out of that."

Then it was her turn to be baffled. "What do you mean?"

He unclenched his jaw enough to say, "My team has this idiotic ritual where every time one of us finds his mate, they run her through the wringer to make sure she truly loves them and will stand by them and is brave and worthy. I warned the rest of them not to do it to you, but I forgot to warn Destiny."

Grace was first annoyed, then had to laugh. "That explains why she seemed so pleased that I was upset. That was a world-class guilt trip. But I guess it proved that I cared how you felt."

"I don't care why she did it," Rafa said angrily. "I don't want my team laying guilt trips on you or trying to scare you or any of that other crap they do."

"I have to ask. Did you haze your teammates' mates?" Grace asked. Rafa looked so cornered that she burst out laughing. "You did! I guess turnaround's fair play. Let them haze me. Destiny only got to me because I didn't know what she was doing. Now that I know it's coming, it won't bother me."

"I hope so. I do want to introduce you to my team. I've met your people—your co-workers, at least—but you haven't met mine."

"I've met Paris," Grace pointed out. "I guess she's both of our people. So why *did* you get married, if it wasn't to keep up her cover?"

Rafa let out a deep sigh that vibrated through his chest. "Because we both thought we'd never be loved."

CHAPTER THIRTEEN

Rafa

Rafa could hardly believe he'd said that. It was his deepest, darkest secret—the thing he'd never confessed to anyone. Even Paris didn't know all the details.

But instead of looking at him with pity, his mate's eyes were full of sympathy and love. It filled him with warmth and strength. So that was what it meant to have a mate. You could jump without a parachute, and know that they would always be there to catch you.

"My family—my lion pride—finds their mates young or not at all," Rafa said. "My grandparents met and married before they were twenty. The rest, by the time they were twenty-five. Mostly their mates were lions from other prides, but sometimes they were other types of shifters. Mate recognition starts working in your late teens or early twenties. Every now and then shifters who fought like cats and dogs when they were kids meet again when they're adults, and boom."

"Boom is right," Grace remarked. "My head's still spinning."

He kissed her. "Mine too. Anyway, when my older sisters were eighteen and twenty and still unmated, my family started introducing them to different shifter families. It was to find them mates, not me—I was too young, I was just fifteen—but I came along. My little sisters too. My parents figured the younger kids could make friends, and who knows, maybe one would turn out to be their mate later."

"All lions?"

"No, we ran through the local prides pretty fast. That summer we all drove up to meet a back-to-nature bear clan in the woods north of Santa Martina. They lived in log cabins and didn't drive cars. My family comes from old money, and I was learning how to behave at white tie balls when I was twelve. And there I was, getting introduced to girls who hunted deer, smoked the venison, tanned the hide, and sewed it into moccasins."

Grace poked him. "You snob."

"Not at all!" Rafa protested. "They were fun. But the one I really hit it off with was a boy my age, Hal. He and I had something in common: neither of us fit in with our family. Hal's clan wanted him to get married and live off the land, and my pride wanted me to get married and live off our investments. But Hal and I needed danger and excitement. We wanted to join the military, but our families were dead-set against it. When we pushed it, they threatened to disinherit us."

"Yikes," Grace remarked. "I don't fit into my family either, but they've never done worse than ground me when I was a teenager and nag me as an adult."

"*Now* they just nag me," said Rafa. "Well, none of us found our mates, but Hal and I stayed in touch. When we were seventeen, we ran off and enlisted in the Navy, and we got on the same SEAL team. It was great—everything we'd wanted. I forgot about mates. I was gone on missions all the time and that's no good for a real relationship. When the pride nagged me about it getting late for me to find my mate, I blew them off."

He hadn't realized that he'd stopped talking until Grace prompted him with, "Until…?"

He let out a deep sigh. "Until I realized that everyone in the pride who hadn't found their mate by my age never found them at all." Even though it had been a long time ago and he'd found his mate after all, he couldn't help wincing at the memory.

"Ouch." She gave his shoulders a comforting squeeze. "I used to worry that I'd never find anyone. That was bad enough without thinking I had an actual deadline."

He relaxed at her touch. "The pride held out hope till I was twenty-eight. Then they gave up on me finding my mate, and started telling me to find some woman I liked well enough and marry her, so I could at least have kids and carry on the family name. But I didn't want to stick some poor woman with a husband who could never truly love her."

"You're a good guy."

Rafa sighed again. "Mostly I tried not to think about it. Then I got an email about my ten-year high school reunion. So I went, hoping against hope that I'd find my mate there. I didn't. But I did find Paris. We'd always hit it off, and we still did. The reunion was terrible—a bunch of people neither of us had ever liked, bragging about how successful and skinny they were. I joked that we should go to Vegas instead, and Paris said, 'Let's do it.'"

"Ah-ha," said Grace.

"We drove for seven hours and got there at midnight. And then we started drinking. I think I had five shots for every one Paris had. We got hammered. Pretty soon we were talking about our nonexistent love lives and crying on each other's shoulders. Metaphorically speaking," he added quickly. "For me, anyway."

"It's all right to cry, you know. It doesn't make you less of a man."

The pride would disagree with that. But maybe Grace was right. He nodded and went on, "We told each other as much of the truth as we could stand to, I guess. I didn't tell her about shifters. But I did say that my family was pressuring me to get married and I'd never even been in love, and I didn't think I ever would be."

He wished he could go back in time and tell his younger self to be patient. That he finally had fallen in love, and it was worth waiting for.

"Paris told me her family was pressuring her to get married too," he went on. "They didn't know about her, you see. She said she was afraid that if it got out, her family would disown her and it would ruin her career. We talked about how depressed we were that we could never have what we really wanted. And we agreed that the best thing to do was to marry someone we at least liked as a person, even if they weren't the love of our lives, so our families would be happy." He hesitated, then admitted, "And so we wouldn't be so lonely."

Grace squeezed his hand.

"And I said, 'Let's do it,'" Rafa concluded.

"And then you noticed the Elvis Wedding Chapel next door?"

"You think you're kidding, but that's exactly what happened." In a lighter tone, he said, "Now you know my tackiest secret. I was married by an Elvis impersonator in a rhinestone-studded jumpsuit. It started sinking in what a terrible mistake we'd made when instead of singing a love song, he serenaded us with 'You Ain't Nothin' But A Hound Dog.'"

Grace snickered. "Seriously?"

"Seriously. And then Paris and I staggered off to a hotel room. All of a sudden we felt stone cold sober. I said, 'Paris, I like you as a friend, but I'm not in love with you. I can't do this.' And Paris said, 'Rafa, you're a great guy. But you're a *guy.* I can't do this."

"Not exactly a match made in heaven. How long did you stay married?"

"Twenty-four hours. We passed out for about twelve, and then it took us a while to recover from our hangovers enough to go out and find someone to divorce us. Not Elvis! Just a guy in a suit. Paris went straight home and told her family she was never going to marry any man. They were upset at first, but by now they're nagging her to meet a nice woman and marry her." Rafa sighed. "There you go. That's the story."

"Thanks for telling me. Poor Paris. Poor you. I'm glad you're both happier now." Grace gave him a puzzled glance. "I don't get why it's this huge secret, though. I know Paris was worried about her career. But why is it such a big deal for you?"

The words caught in his throat, but he managed to force them out. "It's not what happened that's the big deal. It's what I thought it meant. When I went to Vegas, I'd never loved any woman. Not Hal's cousins, not the shifter women my family kept shoving at me, not the women I met in the Navy, not anyone. Paris was beautiful and sexy and kind, and I liked her a lot. But I didn't love her. And when I had to admit that, it convinced me that I wasn't capable of that sort of love. That there was something wrong with me, like I had a hole where my heart ought to be."

"Oh, Rafa," Grace said softly, with all her love for him shining from her beautiful eyes. "There's nothing wrong with you. Nothing at all. There never has been."

"I know. *Now,* I know that." He'd been so afraid to make that final confession, but now that he had, it didn't weigh him down any more. He felt light as a feather. Like Fiona had said, he was walking on air.

"You know, I had it all planned out how I was going to tell you that story. I'd meant to do it while we were cuddling on a bed covered in rose petals after we'd made love, not sitting on a fake Mars rock after we'd had a huge fight. I had champagne and candles and music and everything."

"A bed covered in rose petals?" Grace echoed, and laughed. "Sorry, Rafa. I'm not laughing at you. Exactly. Your date night sounds awesome. And knowing you, I'm sure they'd be the *best* roses and candles and champagne."

"Well, of course."

She ruffled his hair. "Here's the thing, though: you don't need any of that stuff. Sure, it's nice. But you don't have to be this perfectly suave romantic hero. I like *you,* Rafa. Not roses. Not champagne and candles. *You.* I like the guy who fixes the BARF sign and watches me solder and hates rose-flavored cupcakes. You love me for being me—I love you for being you."

Rafa was taken aback. All he could manage was, "Oh."

"Where did that even come from, anyway? You're so good-looking and tall and strong, and you used to be a Navy SEAL. Women must've been falling all over you for your entire life. What makes you feel like you have to go way above and beyond to make them like you?"

"It's a lion thing, partly. We're the king of beasts, everything should be the best for us and the best for our mates. But, honestly, once I thought I was never going to have a mate, I decided to be the coolest single guy ever. Show the world how much I liked it better that way. I didn't want anyone to think I was this lonely guy and feel sorry for me."

"Yeah, being pitied is the worst. I hate it too. After Dean cheated on me and ended up in jail, I could feel people thinking, 'Oh poor Grace, such bad luck with men, so sad.' And 'Oh that Grace, she must be doing *something* to attract that sort of man.'"

"You didn't do a thing. It *was* bad luck. But I don't feel sorry for you. Look at the fantastic mate you have now!"

As Rafa had intended, Grace laughed. "True. Hey, do you still have the rose petals and champagne and stuff at your place?"

"I do. Want to try them out before the petals wilt?"

"Absolutely."

Grace turned off the lights, and they left the theatre. Destiny had taken off when Rafa had arrived, reporting that she'd seen no sign of danger. He scanned the area, but he didn't see anything either. They were alone on an empty street. The night was dark and colder than ever. Grace shivered.

"Take my coat." Rafa slipped it from his shoulders and bent to put it on her.

As he started to straighten, his sharp lion's eyes caught a far-off glint of light at the roof of an otherwise unlit building.

Moonlight on a rifle barrel.

There was no time for a warning. Rafa hit the ground rolling, Grace caught up in his arms. Her startled yelp was drowned out by the crack of a gunshot.

Fragments of concrete struck him in the face, but he was glad of the pain. It told him that the bullet had missed.

That his mate was unhurt.

He rolled again. Another gunshot. More chips of the sidewalk struck him, this time on his hands and arms.

Even as he moved, he was calculating the position of the sniper, the distance between them, and the range of his own handgun. Rafa could try to hit the sniper, but at that distance and moving, it would take a one-in-a-million shot.

As he threw himself to the side one more time, he fired at that glint of light.

Rafa had no idea if he'd hit the sniper or not. The next instant, they landed hard, inside the thick concrete walls of the parking structure. Safe.

For now.

Rafa leaped to his feet, still holding Grace close to his chest. Shielding her with his body, he bolted for his car. He wrenched open the door and lifted her into the passenger seat, then jumped into the driver's seat.

His heart pounding, he turned to look at Grace. Her eyes were huge and her olive skin had gone ashen with fright, but she was alive and unharmed. As far as he could tell, she hadn't even been bruised.

His relief was so intense that it made his head swim. "Thank God."

But he couldn't let himself get distracted. He slammed on the locks, started the car, and floored it out of there, putting the several-story parking structure between them and the probably-still-alive sniper.

There was very little traffic late on a winter night. Rafa broke all the speed limits as he drove, with one hand on the steering wheel and the other dialing his cell phone. He first called 911, as the police could get there faster than his teammates. The police assured him that they'd dispatch SWAT to go after the sniper, and send officers to check on everyone else involved in the play.

He didn't know if the attack had been directed at him or at Grace, or if the sniper might try again. But he'd feel better knowing that everyone connected with the play had police headed their way. He'd have preferred to send his teammates to guard them, but there were far too many *Mars* people, all at their individual homes, for that to be possible.

"Is there a list of them all?" the dispatcher asked.

Rafa turned to Grace. "Have you got everyone's numbers?"

"Of course." She turned on her phone. "If you give me the police email, I'll send them our contact sheet. It has names, addresses, and emergency contacts."

Rafa got the email address, and Grace forwarded the list. A moment later, the dispatcher remarked, "Wow. Someone was well-prepared. Okay, I'm dispatching them now."

Rafa then called Hal, who first made sure they weren't injured, then told him to come straight to the office.

"Thanks. We'll be right there." Rafa hung up. He turned again to Grace and put a hand on her shoulder. "How are you doing?"

"Forget me," she said impatiently. "You're hurt! I've been trying and trying to get your attention."

When he thought back on the last few minutes, he vaguely recalled it. But he'd been intent on talking to the police and Hal. "No, I wasn't hit. Believe me, I'd have noticed."

"You're bleeding!"

Realizing what she must be seeing, he said, "It's nothing. The bullet hit the sidewalk and some bits of cement hit me, that's all."

Grace stretched out a trembling hand and touched his cheek, swiping at some of the stinging cuts. "Oh. Yeah, you're right. They're shallow."

"Like shaving cuts," he assured her. "And I'm a shifter. We heal fast, remember? You watch. They'll close in a few more minutes, and they'll be gone by morning."

"Oh." She visibly relaxed, then shook her head in amazement, sending her purple curls bouncing. "I still can't believe you can turn into a lion. And my cousin can turn into a tiger. For the first time in my life, I'm not going to be the weirdest person in the room."

"You definitely won't be. I'm taking you to meet my team."

Grace gave him a shaky but real smile. "This should be interesting."

"If they haze you, I could turn into a lion and bite them," he offered.

"Nah. Forewarned is forearmed. They can lay all the guilt trips they like, it won't bother me."

He was going to warn her that they could do much more than that when his phone rang.

It was Hal. Rafa put him on speakerphone. "The cops just called me. SWAT found a dead sniper on the roof. It was a one-in-a-million shot, but you got him."

Rafa relaxed, but only a little. For all he knew, there was more than one gunman. "Do they know who he was?"

"Yeah," said Hal. "A professional assassin on the FBI's most wanted list. Looks like you're getting another medal."

"*Another* medal?" Grace echoed. "How many do you have?"

"Enough to weigh down his dress blues," Hal said, at the same time Rafa said, "It's not important. Hal, did the police say if there were any clues about who hired the guy?"

"Didn't look like it," Hal replied. "It'd be someone high up in organized crime, though. You don't find assassins like that on Craig's List."

"And the *Mars* people?" Rafa asked urgently. "Paris?"

"Paris is fine," Hal replied. "An officer is with her now. He says the NASA consultant is there too. They're still tracking down a couple people, but it looks like the only attack was on you and Grace."

"Thanks. I'm on my way." Rafa hung up.

The only attack was on me and *Grace?* He wondered. *Or on me* or *Grace?*

"Which one of us do you think the shooter was after?" Grace asked, as if she'd read his mind.

"I was just wondering that," Rafa replied. "Who's more essential to *Mars,* the bodyguard or the stage manager?"

"You are," she said after a moment's thought.

Surprised, he said, "From what I've seen, the show would fall apart without *you.*"

"I don't think so. Yeah, things would go wrong and it wouldn't run as well, but if I was…" Grace shuddered. "…out of the picture, Carl could step in. But you're the only protection we have. Sure, the police are guarding us now, but how long is that going to last?"

"Probably just tonight," Rafa admitted. "That's why bodyguards exist."

"There you go. I think that shooter was after *you.*"

"I sure hope so."

She stared at him. "What?"

"Better me than you."

"What?!" she repeated. "No!"

"I heal fast," he reminded her. "I'm hard to kill. I have faster reflexes and better vision. Not to mention military training. I turn into a lion. Plus, lots of people have tried to kill me. I'm used to it. And you notice I'm still here. It's much better if any assassination attempts are aimed at me."

"I still don't like it," Grace muttered, but seemed to accept his reasoning.

And if anyone's going to give their life, better me than you, he thought.

It was bad enough that she had nearly been caught in the crossfire of an attack aimed at him. The thought of his mate being the target filled him with protective fury.

"I'll be fine," he promised her. "Don't worry about me. We're going to catch whoever's behind this before they try again. I'll get my entire team on it."

With perfect timing, Rafa pulled into the underground parking lot of Protection, Inc. as he spoke. He got out and opened the door for her. "Sorry for flinging you into the car."

"If someone's shooting at me, you have permission to fling all you like." She stepped out and took his hand. "Guess it's time to meet the family."

CHAPTER FOURTEEN

Grace

Grace still felt shaky as she and Rafa got in the Protection, Inc. elevator. She'd been through a lot of nerve-wracking situations as a stage manager, from a fire effect going wrong and burning off the leading lady's eyebrows to having a black cat suddenly run across the stage in the middle of a performance. Living in Florida had gotten her used to hurricanes, tropical storms, floods, tornados, wildfires, and alligators. Not to mention discovering that her boyfriend was a criminal.

But she'd never been in a situation where anyone's life had been threatened, or been involved in anything more violent than helping to restrain a furious actor whose co-star had decided that it would add a welcome touch of realism to the show if he made a fake slap into a real one.

Rafa's handsome face was streaked with blood, his usually-perfect hair sticky with it. But his arm was strong around her waist. He'd reacted like lightning to shield her, before she'd even realized anything was wrong. She ought to be terrified. But with her mate beside her, she felt protected and safe.

The elevator door opened with a *ding,* and they stepped into the lobby.

Grace had expected it to be packed with a menacing crowd of Rafa's teammates, all just waiting to throw the worst they could manage at her. But the lobby only held two women, both as short and curvy as Grace herself. They gave Grace and Rafa friendly smiles.

"Hi," said the one with curling sandy hair and blue-green eyes. "I'm Ellie McNeil. I'm married to Hal, Rafa's boss. Pleased to meet you."

No sooner had Grace shaken her hand than the other woman, who had straight black hair and brown eyes, seized it. "And I'm Catalina Mendez, one of Rafa's teammates."

Here it comes, Grace thought, and braced herself for the hazing. But Catalina simply said, "I'm also a paramedic. So is Ellie. Are you hurt?"

"No, but Rafa is. You should take care of him."

"I don't need a paramedic for a few tiny cuts," he began.

Catalina stood on her tiptoes, grabbed him by the shoulders, and shoved him down on the sofa. "Maybe not, but you're getting one anyway." She opened a medical bag and began to check him over.

"Have a seat," Ellie said to Grace, and indicated the sofa.

Grace sat down beside Rafa, who was rolling his eyes as Catalina applied antiseptic wipes to his face.

"I'm fine," Rafa protested.

"Sometimes people get such an adrenaline rush that they don't even notice that they're hurt," Catalina said. "So sit tight and let us check you. The less you argue, the sooner you'll be done."

Grace liked the paramedics already. They were obviously concerned for Rafa. She sat still and let Ellie inspect her for injuries, then take her pulse and listen to her heart. Maybe the whole hazing thing was overblown. Rafa had said he'd warned off everyone but Destiny, so probably that guilt trip was all of the gauntlet Grace would have to run.

Relaxing, she glanced around the lobby. It wasn't what she'd expected from a bodyguard agency. She'd imagined sleek and uncomfortable furniture made of steel and plastic, walls lined with testimonials from grateful famous clients plus photos of the bodyguards looking tough, and brochures with titles like *Home Security for the Wealthy and Paranoid* and *Protecting Your Pooch.*

There were no brochures of any kind, only a rack of magazines with pretty pictures, like *National Geographic* and *American Wildlife*. The sofa was made of dark wood and black leather, and the rest of the furniture matched it. The floor was polished hardwood. A table held bowls of old-fashioned movie candy like Jordan almonds and Junior Mints and Sugar Babies. Beautiful orchids grew in pots on the windowsills. The effect was professional, but also cozy and reassuring—which,

Grace supposed, was exactly what a bodyguard agency probably wanted to convey.

But it was the pictures on the wall that captured her attention. They were big color photos of animals in their natural habitats: a pride of lions, a wolf, a grizzly bear…

"Ah-ha!" Grace exclaimed, and poked Rafa in the ribs. "Those are you guys, right? You're the lion!"

"You got it," Rafa said.

"I'm the leopard." Catalina pointed out her photo.

Grace looked at it, then back at the woman. On first glance, it was hard to imagine. On second glance, there *was* something feline about Catalina, much as Rafa's movements embodied a lion's confidence and power.

"It shouldn't have taken everyone else this long to get here," Rafa said suddenly. "Where are they?"

"Right here."

The voice came out of nowhere. Grace leaped up from the sofa, her heart slamming into her ribs.

A man was standing right there in the middle of the room. A deadly man—a terrifying man—the hit man come to kill Rafa!

Grace shouted at the top of her theatre-trained lungs, "RAFA! GET HIM!"

And then, to distract the hit man, she snatched up the nearest object—a bowl of Reese's Pieces—and hurled it at his head.

The hit man ducked. Reese's Pieces flew all over the office, and the wooden bowl bounced off the wall and smashed an orchid pot. Rafa grabbed the hit man and slammed him into the wall.

"Ow," remarked the hit man.

"How dare you!" Rafa shouted, his cheeks dark with fury. "This is the worst yet!"

The hit man seemed completely unruffled, either by the yelling or the slamming. "Oh, I wouldn't say that. Lucas *hissed* at my mate. That was the worst, right, Catalina?"

"Actually, I think the worst is what Fiona said to Raluca," Catalina put in. "She implied that Raluca cared more about her designer dresses than she did about her mate."

"Hmm." Ellie scratched her head. "That's meaner, but Fiona implying that Journey was a gold-digger was ruder. Fiona still wins."

By then Grace had figured it out. "Rafa? This is the dragon guy, right?"

"No, this jerk is Shane, a panther shifter," Rafa replied. "Lucas is the dragon."

Puzzled, Grace said, "But you said dragon shifters are the ones who can turn invisible."

"Only when they're actual dragons," explained Shane over Rafa's shoulder.

Shane made a quick movement, too fast for Grace to see exactly what he'd done, and extracted himself from Rafa's grip. He picked his way across the floor, avoiding the Reese's Pieces, and offered Grace his hand. "Shane Garrity. Pleased to meet you."

More baffled than angry, she shook it. "Grace Chang. What's with the invisibility?"

"It's not really invisibility," Shane explained. "It's unnoticeability. If any of you had thought to look for me, you'd have seen me."

That hardly answered Grace's question. She tried again. "How come you can do it, though? Is it a panther thing? I guess camouflage would be useful for a predator."

Shane's ice-blue eyes flickered, and his mouth tightened. It was only for a second, and then his cool expression returned. But Grace knew what she'd seen. She didn't know how or why, but she'd gotten to him.

"Yeah, something like that," he said, a beat too late. "You're brave, though. Good reflexes. And you trust your mate. Well done."

A woman's voice called out, "Shane, sweep up those Reese's Pieces before everyone stomps them into the floor!"

Grace turned. A door had opened while she'd been distracted. A woman with platinum-blonde hair and clear green eyes stood framed in the doorway, with more people crowded behind her. The blonde woman tossed Shane a broom and dustpan. He caught them neatly, and began to sweep.

Ellie and Catalina burst into giggles. Grace was still more confused than amused, but had to laugh when she saw Shane sweep out a candy-free path to the door, so the others could come crowding in.

"Not okay, Shane," Rafa growled. "Not okay, everyone! I can't believe you all got in on it. Ellie and Catalina, even! And you know what it feels like."

"Hal talked me into it," Ellie said. "Blame him."

"Shane talked me into it," Catalina said. "You can blame me, though. Once he explained what he wanted to do, I thought it would be too funny not to go along with it."

Rafa glared at her. "After Grace got shot at?"

Unrepentant, Catalina said, "I figured it would cheer her up, once she realized what was going on. Come on, it was hilarious! And if she can't take some teasing, then she's not a good mate for you anyway."

Grace checked for stray candies underfoot, then went and caught Rafa's arm. "It's okay. I forgive them. They were just trying to look out for you, in a very strange way. And hey, you were right: I'm nowhere near the weirdest one in the room."

Catalina and Ellie snickered again.

"You're right about that," Rafa muttered, but seemed to cool off.

"That is, I forgive them if that's it," Grace added. She looked around the room, catching everyone's eyes. "It is, right? No more hilarious little surprises?"

"Nope. That was it. We decided to all go in on Shane's test. You pass." The man who spoke was burlier than Rafa and an inch or two taller, with brown hair and hazel eyes. He held out his hand. "I'm Hal Brennan. Welcome to Protection, Inc."

After that, the others crowded around.

The blonde woman introduced herself as Fiona Payne. Grace shook her hand, wondering if what Catalina and Ellie had said about her had been part of the hazing or was actually true. Fiona seemed perfectly friendly, but there was something about her cool green eyes that made Grace suspect that it was true.

"I am Lucas, and I am very honored to meet you." The young man with a gold chain around his throat offered her his hand with the slightest awkwardness, as if it was a greeting he wasn't quite accustomed to. His hand was very hot when she shook it, as if he'd come in from a blazing summer day rather than a cold winter night.

Nick, still in his black leather jacket, offered her an apology as well as a handshake. "Sorry about today. I had no fucking clue Rafa hadn't told you he got married by Elvis. I mean, I also had no fucking clue you even existed."

"Nick…" Rafa began.

Guessing that he wasn't thrilled either by the reminder or the language, Grace caught both their eyes and replied, "Don't fucking worry about it."

Nick laughed. After a moment, Rafa chuckled.

At last, Grace and Destiny came face to face.

"So, apparently we're related," Grace said.

"We're cousins, yeah," Destiny said, nodding.

"Did you always know that?"

Destiny shook her head. "Nope. I figured it out just now, when you told Shane your full name. I'd heard you were in Santa Martina and I knew you were doing something in theatre, but I didn't put it together till then. Sorry I never looked you up."

"Sorry *I* never looked *you* up," Grace replied.

"Well, here we are now. One more for the girls' club!" Destiny glanced at Fiona. "We outnumber the boys now."

It took Grace a moment to put her words and glance together. Once she did, she realized what it meant: all the men had found their mates. Only Destiny and Fiona were still alone. Destiny had spoken cheerfully and Fiona hadn't reacted at all, but Grace wondered if they were lonely.

Hal's deep voice cut through the chatter. "Everyone, come on in to the board room. We need to discuss how we're going to protect Grace and her show."

Rafa led Grace into a room with a bunch of chairs grouped around a large table. There were sandwiches and sodas on the table, which came as a relief to Grace. She hadn't eaten anything all day after breakfast but a pair of cupcakes. She and the bodyguards ate as Rafa got them up to speed on the situation with *Mars: The Musical.*

When he was finished, Fiona said, "Rafa asked me to look into the possibility that someone involved with *My Fair Lady* is behind this. An amateur could have bribed someone working on *Mars* to sabotage it. But this murder attempt was professional. So if it is someone from *My Fair Lady*, my guess is that the show is backed by organized crime. I think the best way to find out is for me to go undercover over there."

"Go for it," Hal said. "Though I'm wondering if the plot might have succeeded already."

"What do you mean?" asked Grace.

Rafa was the one who explained. "Up till now, you and Paris were the only people working on *Mars* who believed that anything dangerous was happening. Now everyone knows—and they know it could cost them their lives. They might just quit."

"*You* could quit," Hal said. "Think about it. Is this show worth risking your life? You could find another job…"

Grace didn't need to think about it. Indignantly, she said, "I'm not getting run off my own show. It's not about the money. It's the principle of the thing. The show must go on!"

"Let's hope everyone else feels that way," said Hal.

"Couldn't this be the end of it, though?" Grace asked. "The person who shot at us is dead. Maybe he was the same person who arranged the accidents inside the theatre. I'd been thinking it was someone working on the show, but it could have been someone who snuck in and out without anyone noticing. If it was just one man and he's dead, maybe whoever hired him will just give up."

"Maybe," said Hal. "But we need to take some precautions in case they don't. Rafa can protect everyone while they're all at the theatre, and he can stay with you wherever you go. But we've already had one attack outside of the theatre, and there's over thirty people working on the show. I can't assign bodyguards to all of them."

Grace's heart sank. It seemed like an impossible task. But when she glanced around the table, she saw that nobody looked particularly worried. Instead, they all leaned forward, nodding, as if this was a situation they'd encountered before.

"Fiona will be working elsewhere," Hal went on. "I can get the whole team out tomorrow morning to make sure there's no more snipers. But after that, the rest of us will be on other assignments. So…"

"Invisible Man?" asked Rafa.

Hal nodded. "You got it. Now, here's how we'll run it…"

The bodyguards spent hours reviewing the situation and the best plan for dealing with it, periodically asking Grace for details on how the show was run and the personalities of the people in it. By the end of the meeting, she felt reassured. More, she felt at home. Hazing aside, the team was as professional and organized as even a stage manager could desire, and like one, they carefully worked out everything that could possibly go wrong and figured out what to do to avoid it or, if they couldn't assure that, what to do if it happened.

Once the team had figured out their overall plan and were working on the details, Grace went to the other end of the room and started calling everyone from *Mars*, making sure they were safe, telling them that the rehearsal tomorrow was still on and they'd be protected there too, and doing her best to reassure them.

Paris asked her if she'd worked things out with Rafa, and sounded happy when Grace said that she had. Melissa asked about "that repulsive rodent," and sounded disappointed when Grace assured her that Tycho was fine. Carl wanted to know if Grace was all right, Lubomir gloomily remarked that he'd thought all the American movies where people have shoot-outs in the streets were fiction, and Brady said he was glad she'd called, as after thinking it over, he'd realized that he just didn't like strawberry jello. He asked her if it could be switched to cherry.

At the end of the meeting, Hal suggested that Grace and Rafa spend the night at Protection, Inc. rather than returning to his apartment or hers.

"It's more secure," Hal explained.

"We have bedrooms," Rafa assured her.

"And spare clothes," added Destiny. "I'll loan you some of mine. We look about the same size."

Everyone else departed, leaving Grace and Rafa alone in the building.

"I meant to show you around," he said. "I think you'd love our tech room. But it's getting late…"

"Getting?" Grace yawned. "Excuse me."

"Definitely late."

Rafa led her to a small bedroom that was almost completely taken up with a big bed. They undressed and climbed in. Grace curled into his comforting warmth. Her eyelids felt swollen and heavy. She was used to staying up late, but she felt crushingly exhausted.

"Sorry I'm too tired…" she murmured.

He pulled her closer, letting her pillow her head on his shoulder. "Don't worry about it. Getting shot at takes a lot out of you. Besides, we've got plenty of nights to come, right?"

She wasn't sure if she answered him aloud or not. But the thought of plenty of nights with Rafa sent her straight into a deep and pleasant sleep.

*

If Grace had been asked to guess how she'd feel the morning after she'd thought she'd been lied to by the man she loved, then worked the rest of the day, then survived a murder attempt, then got scared half to death, she'd have said, "Terrible."

But when she opened her eyes the next morning, she was filled with a sense of contentment, even renewal. She lay enfolded in Rafa's arms, safe and sound. He was still asleep, with his sleek hair falling across her face and his. The covers had been pushed aside, and his muscular body seemed poured across the bed in total relaxation. And yet she was certain that if there was any danger, he'd be up and ready to fight on her behalf before she could blink.

Testing, she whispered, "Rafa?"

Her voice was so soft that a person standing in the door of the small room wouldn't have heard her. But he instantly opened his eyes, alert but unalarmed, and said, "I want to wake up next to you every morning for the rest of my life."

Grace still wasn't used to all that love directed at her. It was like she'd been a flower planted in the desert, and suddenly the heavens had opened up and rain had poured down, giving her everything she needed to grow.

She swallowed. "Me too."

Next thing she knew, he was out of bed and scooping her into his arms. She squeaked in surprise, then relaxed and let him carry her into the shower.

There's nothing in the world that feels as good as having hot water pour down on you while the man you love shampoos your hair, Grace thought as he did exactly that. *Except waking up in his arms. And having sex with him.*

Now that her life contained Rafa, an endless vista of "No, *this* is the best" moments stretched out in front of her.

When he was done with her hair, she got him to sit down so she could do the same to him. She inspected the choices of shampoo and conditioner curiously. "These are awfully nice for the spare room in a security agency. Did you pick them so you'd always have something good for your mane?"

With absolutely no self-consciousness, he replied, "Yes."

Grinning, Grace worked the fancy shampoo through his hair. It slid through her fingers like silk. She teased him, "Did you decorate the office too?"

"No, Fiona and Hal did that. She did the whole thing originally, except for the photos on the wall. Those were Hal's idea. But she used to have a white sofa and white carpeting, until Hal switched to black leather and hardwood floors."

"More masculine?"

"Easier to clean. Nick ruined two sofas in a row, and then Hal put his foot down."

"What did he do, spill beer on them?"

Rafa looked up at her, his dark eyes serious. "No. Blood."

Unsettled, Grace didn't ask for more details. She wasn't sure she wanted to know. But there was something else she couldn't resist asking about. "Destiny said you got your arm slashed open by a gangster and bled all over the floor. When you said she was hazing me, I thought you meant she'd made up the whole story. Did she?"

"No. She told it to mess with you, but it's a true story. It happened right after Nick wrecked the sofa the second time. That was it for Fiona's 'snowy mountains' color scheme." Rafa spoke lightly, but Grace didn't miss the way he was watching her.

"I'm not going to run screaming, if that's what you're thinking," she said. "It is scary, though. How often do you guys get hurt?"

"Hardly ever," he assured her. "That is, it's hardly ever anything serious. Little cuts like I got last night, sure. But you can see those are gone now."

He tipped up his face for her inspection. Sure enough, she couldn't even see where they had been. Then he displayed his arm, tracing a line down his bulging biceps. "See? That's from memory. There's no scar."

"How'd the gangster get the drop on you with a knife, anyway?"

"It wasn't a knife, it was a saber-tooth tiger fang." Rafa shrugged. "And, well, that's how. I was expecting a shifter, but not that kind of shifter. I didn't even know they existed. It caught me by surprise, and then *he* caught me by surprise."

Grace eyed him suspiciously, wondering if he was pulling her leg. "Uh-huh. A saber-tooth tiger. A saber-tooth tiger *gangster*."

"You know a dragon," he pointed out. "And a werewolf ex-gangster."

"That doesn't surprise me," she remarked. "Nick has 'gone straight' written all over him. Okay. I'll believe the saber-tooth tiger gangster."

They turned off the shower and got dressed. Destiny had thoughtfully provided clothing in as close to Grace's style as she could manage. As she put on the black lace dancing dress, she thought again about what Rafa had said.

"You said you hardly ever got seriously hurt on the job," Grace said. "How often is 'hardly ever?'"

"I never have. Neither has Catalina. Or Fiona. Or Destiny. Well, Destiny might argue that one. Before Nick switched sides, he bit her deep enough to leave a scar. She's never let him forget it. But that's just because it shows when she wears a tank top." Rafa stopped talking, and his smile faded.

"What about the rest of you?"

"Hal got shot once," he admitted. "So did Shane. Nick… It's a long story, but he got hurt badly enough that it took him a month to recover. And Lucas got poisoned and nearly died."

"Poisoned!" She stared at him. "How did that happen?"

"That's another long story." Rafa's dark gaze settled on her, serious and intense. "Short version is, he was protecting his mate. That's what happened to all of them. They weren't careless, but I guess they were less willing to protect themselves if there was even a chance of their mate getting hurt instead. I didn't quite understand that before, but I do now."

"I don't want you to get yourself killed to prevent me from getting scratched!" Grace burst out.

Rafa seemed taken aback. "That's not what I meant. Their mates' lives were in danger."

"I don't want you to sacrifice yourself for me," she repeated, because it didn't seem to be sinking in.

He folded his arms across his chest. Stubbornness radiated from every inch of him, like he was some immovable boulder. "Protecting you is my job. And my heart. I can't promise that."

Frustrated, she said, "What do you think it'll do to *my* heart if you take a bullet for me? Rafa, imagine how you'd feel if I did it for you!"

Instantly, he said, "Don't do it for me!" Then he seemed to replay his words in his mind. With audible reluctance, he said, "I'll take care of myself *too.*"

That was obviously as far as he'd go, so she had to accept that.

Love is scary, she thought as they set out for the theatre. *Even if you trust the person you love. You just switch from being scared that they'll betray you to being scared that they'll take a bullet for you.*

All the same, she wouldn't trade Rafa and his selfless courage for anything. To think that she'd tried to talk herself into dating Carl, just because she was lonely and he was a nice guy who liked her. That would have been as much of a disaster as Rafa's Vegas marriage.

You can't force a relationship, Grace thought. *There's no substitute for love.*

They pulled into the parking lot. She couldn't help glancing around nervously as she got out of the car. Hit men could be anywhere...

Rafa also looked around, but with no more than his usual alertness. "Don't forget the plan. My team's been combing the area for hours already. They wouldn't have missed a sniper."

Reassured, Grace walked to the theatre. She unlocked it, and they went straight up to her booth. The nanny cam had been replaced by an elaborate closed-circuit camera system. It also had a monitor that enabled her to see backstage, but the resolution was far better and it was clearly a more reliable system.

"That'll be great for when I run the show. I'll be able to see what's going wrong backstage before anyone even tells me about it." Belatedly, she added, "And see if anyone's trying to kill anyone or sabotage the show, of course."

"I love your priorities," Rafa remarked with a grin.

The actors, musicians, and crew arrived as they climbed down from the booth, all of them nervous and fidgety. Grace called them into a circle.

Rafa explained what had happened, and told them about the closed-circuit cameras and that he would stay on to guard the theatre.

That seemed to relieve them, until a violinist put up her hand. "But Grace got shot at outside the theatre. I know we're safe inside, but what about when we leave? You can't guard all of us."

"Sure we can," said Shane, emerging from the shadows.

Everybody jumped, even Grace, who had known he was going to do that. Melissa let out a shrill scream, and Carl spilled the coffee he'd been handing to Lubomir.

A chorus of "How did you do that?" rose up. Shane stood there, unsmiling and surrounded by a near-palpable air of danger, until the questions died into an uneasy silence.

"That's my teammate Shane," said Rafa. "We call him 'The Invisible Man.'"

Nobody laughed. The people who were nearest to Shane tried to unobtrusively slide farther away.

"You won't see me again." Shane's ice-blue gaze swept over the crowd. A chill of fear came over Grace as it touched her, and she involuntarily drew back. "But I'll see you. If anyone tries to attack you, I'll see them, too."

Without another word, he turned and walked out. Another silence fell as he vanished into the shadows. Everyone glanced around, visibly unnerved.

Grace carefully avoided looking at Rafa. It would ruin her straight face if she did. She just hoped the ploy would work on the person it was actually aimed at—the secret enemy. *She* sure wouldn't risk attacking anyone if she thought Shane was lurking invisibly in the shadows at all times.

"I believe that we'll be safe from now on," Lubomir said. "But I can't make that decision for you. If you don't want to risk working on the show, you're free to leave."

Everyone looked at each other. Grace held her breath. This was the part that worried her. If a few people quit, the show would survive. But if lots of them did, that would be it. The mysterious enemy would have closed down the show.

And then what would happen to her relationship with Rafa? Would he follow her back to Delbert-on-the-Sea? Would she stay in Santa Martina, living off his money because she was unable to support herself? Grace couldn't decide which of those options she hated more. She treasured her independence. But she couldn't force Rafa to leave his job.

Lubomir nodded at Grace.

"Show of hands," she said, her stomach clenching with anxiety. "Who wants to leave?"

Nobody moved. After a moment, Tycho, who was in his usual

position on Ruth's shoulder, gave a loud squeak.

Melissa did too.

"The show must go on!" Paris said. "Even Tycho says so."

Melissa's lip curled as she glared at the rat, but she agreed, "The show must go on!"

"No one chases us off our own show," the props guy declared. "We are *Mars: The Mighty!*"

A chorus of *"Mars: The Mighty!"* arose, then broke off in laughter.

Paris leaned over to pet Tycho, then gave Ruth a pet too. She had obviously either done Ruth's hair herself or given her advice, because it was no longer scraped into a painful-looking bun. Instead, it was in a practical but pretty French braid down her back. Ruth no longer looked cranky, but sat leaning against Paris's side, smiling as she sipped a cup of steaming tea.

Rafa squeezed Grace's hand. "See? Everything's going to work out."

For the first time, she believed it.

When the rehearsal ended, Rafa drove her to his apartment. It was spacious and well-furnished, but impersonal: like "the ideal apartment for a single man" from an article in *GQ*, not a place where a real person lived. The only thing that wasn't perfect was a vase full of dead roses.

Rafa tossed them in the trash. "So much for scattering petals on the bed."

"Some other time." Eyeing the spotless, velvety sofa, Grace asked, "Don't you ever just kick back, order pizza, and eat it while you're watching TV?"

"I do, but I sit on the floor."

"What's the point of a sofa you can't sit on?"

"To impress the mate I was hoping I'd find," he confessed. "Though now that I've found her, I'm realizing that any mate I'd actually want would say exactly what you just did."

Grace flopped down on the sofa, dangling her feet over the arm. "There. Come break it in with me."

Rafa looked down at her with a fire in his dark eyes that kindled an answering heat in her. "Don't move."

He turned the lights down to a soft glow and put on some instrumental music.

He's the romantic one, Grace thought. *Sure, he wants to please me, but he likes it too. I'm the one who eats roses, but he's the one who's disappointed that his roses died.*

But she wanted to please him, too. Sure, she'd have been just as happy having a quickie under the sound board or in the closet, but if Rafa liked soft lights and romantic music, then she had no problem going along with that.

Her breathing grew faster as she watched him undress. She still wasn't used to seeing that powerful male body naked before her, for her to touch and please and be pleased by. A desperate urge seized her to stroke and caress him, from his broad shoulders and muscular arms to the steely hardness of his huge erection.

"Rafa!" She held out her arms to him.

He stepped toward her, his footsteps silent as a cat's. She felt dizzy with desire as he bent over her and stripped her bare. The sofa was soft and velvety against her skin, and his fingers were burning hot. Or maybe she was the one who was burning. He kissed her, his lips and tongue just as hot as the rest of him, and she pulled him in closer.

When he straddled her, she gave an involuntary moan and thrust up until the entire length of his shaft was inside her. She clenched around him as he began to thrust in and out, in an irresistible rhythm. The silk of his skin, the velvet of the sofa, the soft lights, the music—all of it blended together into an atmosphere of overwhelming sensuality.

Now I get it, Grace thought dreamily. *This is what the lights and music are for.*

But that was the last conscious thought she had. After that, she was swept away on a tide of sensation, passion, and love.

"I love you," she gasped as she came. "I love you!"

"I love you," Rafa growled. "My mate!"

A moment later, they were lying together on the thoroughly broken-in sofa. The music was still playing.

"That was wonderful," Grace said with a sigh of contentment. "I've completely changed my opinion about romantic music and soft lighting. It's great. At least, it's great when it's with you." Then, unable to resist teasing him, she added, "Though it would have been even better with rose petals."

"Dammit! I should have stopped and gotten some more on the way here," Rafa burst out. Then she saw him register that she'd been kidding. "You laugh, but some day I *will* cover the bed with rose petals, and then you'll know what you've been missing."

"Some day," Grace said. But she couldn't imagine anything better than what she already had.

CHAPTER FIFTEEN

Rafa

Grace pirouetted for Rafa, making her short skirt flare out. She was all dressed up for opening night in a black dress with gauzy skirts and a heart-shaped corset top, bubblegum-pink stockings printed with tiny black spiders, and black combat boots. Her tumbled purple hair was adorned with a 1950s style hat with a fluttering black mesh veil and a huge black ostrich feather.

The dress showed off her luscious breasts and thighs, the hat called attention to her beautiful face, and the entire outfit made him smile with how quintessentially *Grace* it all was. Where did you even go to shop for pink stockings with little fanged spiders?

"Well?" she asked. "What do you think?"

"You look sexy and adorable. And weird in the very best way," he said with a grin. "That's what you were going for, right?"

"That's what I'm always going for," Grace replied, also smiling.

Rafa ducked into the next room, then returned with a bouquet of bright pink roses in a heavy vase of rough black pottery. He'd thought about how Grace liked to dress, with her signature contrasts of tough and pretty, black and pink, leather and lace, and had tried to replicate that in his opening night gift.

"Happy opening night," he said. "I thought you could put them in your booth."

"Thanks, I will." Grace took the vase, smiling as she hefted its solid weight. "Wow, this is so me. Thanks. The roses match my stockings exactly."

"Minus the spiders," he teased.

"You never know, there might be one or two hiding in there." She breathed in their scent. "This is really it. Big break or big bust. Or…"

"I'll keep you safe," he promised. "The show too. I promise. But nothing's happened since I shot that sniper, and it's been weeks since then. My guess is that whoever was behind the whole thing decided it was too hot to handle and called it off."

"Have you heard anything from Fiona?" Grace asked.

"Nothing different from the last time she checked in," he said with a shrug. "She's still undercover, and she still hasn't found anything. But I promise you, if anyone at *My Fair Lady* is—or was—behind this, she'll catch them. And if they had nothing to do with it, she'll be able to tell us that for sure, too."

That seemed to reassure her. They drove to the theatre, where for once, Grace wasn't the first person to arrive. When they went inside, the theatre was practically buzzing with excitement.

Paris was passing around a platter of cupcakes. "Rafa? Rose for you?"

He made a face, and she laughed and patted his arm. "Or maybe chocolate."

"Later," he said. To his amusement, Grace helped herself to a rose cupcake.

Ruth came in, wearing an elegant black dress and a necklace with a red stone carved into the shape of Mars. Paris gave her a chocolate cupcake, and she gave Paris a bouquet of red roses.

"You don't look fully dressed without Tycho on your shoulder," Paris remarked.

"He had to stay home. I doubt that the rest of the audience would appreciate him the way you do," replied Ruth.

"Looking forward to seeing *Mars* from the audience?" Paris asked.

"Yes, I actually am. It's not as scientifically correct as I'd hoped, but maybe people who see it will be inspired to read up on Mars. And to be honest, if it was more accurate it might be less entertaining."

Paris grinned. "Admit it, Ruth. You love the Martians."

"I don't love the Martians," Ruth said firmly. "They don't exist."

"You never know," Grace put in. "The world can be stranger than you think."

Ruth shot her a dubious look. "That's true in general, but Mars has been very thoroughly scanned. If there were Martians or even Martian artifacts, we'd have long since noticed them. But I'm fine with Paris wearing her hair loose. It's not accurate. But it's very pretty."

"Maybe this show will inspire the next generation of scientists," Paris suggested. "Or astronauts. Just imagine some young person sitting in the audience who'll see me and Brady exploring Mars, and think, 'That's what I want to do for the rest of my life.'"

"Oh, I hope so." Ruth kissed her, then said, "I better get to my seat. Have a great show!"

Paris and Grace looked horrified. Simultaneously, they said, "Don't say that!"

"Why not?" Ruth asked.

"It's a theatre superstition," Grace explained. "It's bad luck to wish for good things to happen on opening night—whatever you wish for, supposedly the opposite will happen. What you say is 'break a leg,' and then they'll have a good show."

"You know superstitions aren't real—" Ruth began.

"Ruth," Paris said warningly.

"All right," said Ruth. "Break a leg, Paris. You too, Grace."

"What about me?" Rafa put in.

Ruth rolled her eyes, but said, "Break a leg, Rafa."

As Ruth headed for the audience, Brady tapped Grace on the shoulder. "About the jello..."

"It's raspberry," Grace said. She'd clearly had it with Brady's complaints about the jello. "And it's homemade this time. I think what you really hate is artificial sweetener. But no matter how it tastes, eat it and act like it's delicious. You're an actor, Brady. So act!"

"Okay. Sure." Brady backed off, looking mildly alarmed. Rafa suppressed a grin. Grace had clearly been repressing that remark for some time.

Rafa accompanied her as she made her rounds, checking to make sure everything was ready and safe.

Carl met her when she inspected the flying mechanism. "I just checked it. No tampering, no frayed wires, absolutely nothing wrong."

"Thanks, Carl," Grace said, but she went on examining it until she'd made sure of that herself. Then she turned back to her assistant. "All right. You're in charge of backstage. Break a leg!"

Carl winked. "Shouldn't that be 'break a wire?'"

"Too soon, Carl," said Grace, shaking her head in mock reproval.

Rafa and Grace went up to her booth, where she placed the vase of roses on a table, then checked the electrical equipment and headphones. As she did so, he checked the closed circuit camera tapes and monitor. The tapes showed nothing out of the ordinary. They never had, ever since they'd been installed.

There haven't been any 'accidents' in weeks, Rafa told himself. *Whoever was behind this obviously gave up when I shot their assassin.*

All the same, he didn't like the fact that he still didn't know who had hired that assassin. With his mate's safety at stake, he wouldn't be able to relax until he'd brought that person to justice.

Fiona will figure it out, he thought. *She's the best at detective work. I'll let her do her job, and I'll do what I do best—protecting my mate.*

Grace nudged him, pointing out the soundproofed window. "Look at that. We sold out!"

She was right. Every seat in the audience was taken.

"And no folding chairs in precarious places," Rafa teased.

"Not with me around, there's not."

As she picked up her headset, he gave her a quick but passionate kiss. "Break a leg."

"You too," she replied.

She ran her fingers through his hair, then took off her hat and put on the headset. He watched as she began to murmur directions to the people backstage, her hands dancing over the light and sound controls. On the monitor, stagehands ran to move scenery and actors scrambled to change costumes; onstage, everything happened smoothly.

As always, the booth was very hot. Rafa took off his jacket and draped it over a chair. He watched Grace with pride as everything unfolded onstage so perfectly at her command. His mate was in her element, making her show a success. And so was he, making sure she was safe. He stood with his back aching from having to stoop in the low-ceilinged room, and sweat trickling down his spine from the heat. He'd never been happier in his life.

CHAPTER SIXTEEN

Fiona

Fiona Payne woke up blindfolded on a cold floor, with her ankles tied together and her hands bound behind her back. Her head ached, and she felt dizzy and nauseated.

I've been drugged, she thought. *Or hit over the head.*

Her thoughts felt slow and sluggish, as if they were swimming in some thick liquid. She forced herself to breathe deeply and concentrate.

What's the last thing I remember...?

Piece by piece, her memories returned. She was undercover on *My Fair Lady*. She'd bribed a stagehand to leave the production, then showed up looking for work and taken his place. But in the weeks she'd spent working on the play itself, she'd become satisfied that nobody she worked with was involved in any plot.

That left the producers, who had offices outside of the theatre. She'd then bribed one of their assistants and taken her place, which enabled her to get access to their computers. But once again, she hadn't found anything suspicious. Then it had occurred to her that men of their generation often weren't very computer-savvy, and might be doing things the old-fashioned way. So she'd decided to do another and more thorough search of the offices themselves.

And she'd found something. One of the producers had a secret drawer in his desk. She'd used the hidden catch to open it...

...and something had pricked her finger.

I was careless, she thought. *I missed a booby trap.*

And someone had found her.

Was he still there?

She lay quietly and listened. Yes. She could hear breathing. Several people breathing. Two? Three? More? She couldn't tell.

Fiona considered her options. She was tied up with rope. If she shifted, her bonds would snap and her blindfold would be pulled or torn off. Normally she'd never shift in front of people who didn't already know about shifters, and she bet her captors didn't, or they'd have used handcuffs and chains just in case. But she'd do it if it was the only way to save her life. Her enemies would look like lunatics if they claimed she'd turned into a leopard. They probably wouldn't say a word for that exact reason.

And if they didn't even know shifters existed, she'd not only have the element of surprise on her side, she'd have the element of *shock.*

On the other hand, she had no idea who she was up against or even how many of them there were. Based on the booby trap and the way she'd been tied up, she faced hardened and experienced criminals. They'd have guns, for sure. Shifters healed fast, but a bullet in the head would kill her as easily as it would kill a human. And any professional gunman confronted with a surprise snow leopard attack would be as likely to shoot and keep shooting as he would to drop the gun in terror.

Lie in wait, hissed her snow leopard. *Let your prey come to you.*

Good plan, Fiona replied silently.

She twitched as if she was just then waking up, then rolled toward her side, hoping to feel the concealed pistol she carried in a thigh holster. But it was gone.

Dammit.

But she wasted no time, but carried on with her plan. Fiona twitched again, then moaned. Making her voice high and shaky, she said, "Hello? Is anyone there? Help me!"

"Cut the bullshit," came an unfamiliar male voice. "We're on to you."

"What?" She tried to sit up, then moaned again. "My head hurts. Why can't I move?"

"I said, cut the bullshit."

Footsteps stalked toward her, and the toe of a boot prodded her in the ribs. Fiona had been expecting that, but she let out a scream. Even if they *did* know who she was, there was no harm letting them think they had her at their mercy.

Play weak, hissed her snow leopard with satisfaction. *Then rip out their throats!*

I'm not ripping out anyone's throat, Fiona replied. *I'm* never *going to rip out anyone's throat. Haven't you figured that out by now?*

Her snow leopard gave a discontented hiss. Clearly, she had not.

Rough hands yanked off her blindfold. Fiona blinked at the bright electric lights. As she'd expected, she was on the floor of the office she'd broken into. Her purse, which contained a cell phone and her other gun, was across the room, far out of her reach. At least no one could use it to identify her; all her IDs were fake, and the phone had no contacts or true information on it.

The producer with the booby-trapped desk, Mr. Moore, stood at the back wall, looking nervous. Sweat shone on his bald head, though the room was cool. He was clearly no threat. But the burly man looming over her, whom she'd never seen before, held his gun like he knew how to use it. And so did the other two men who flanked him. All three had the dead eyes and blank faces of professional killers.

Yep, thought Fiona. *We're* definitely *lying in wait.*

But there was a bright side. Her captors were clearly hit men, which confirmed that *My Fair Lady* was connected with organized crime. Now all she needed to do was find out who their boss was and who he'd sent to sabotage *Mars: The Musical,* and the case would be solved.

But Fiona was having a hard time focusing on the bright side. Unpleasant tingles of fear crept up and down her spine. As a bodyguard, she was used to dangerous situations. She was used to being outnumbered. And she was used to being alone. But when she looked from those dead-eyed men to the barrels of their guns, a memory popped into her mind, so vivid that it felt like she was living it all over again:

Dry leaves crunched underfoot as Fiona ran to rejoin her teammates, adrenaline pumping through her veins, her nerves singing with the fierce joy of a battle fought and a mission accomplished.

Of all her teammates, she was closest to Shane, and she'd been frantic when he'd disappeared. But they'd tracked down his captors, a black ops agency called Apex, and broken him loose. Fiona had personally set the charges that blew up the base he'd been held in, destroying the Apex headquarters so they could never harm him again.

"It's done," she started to call as she reached the grove that was their rendezvous point. "I blew up the—"

And then she saw Shane, sprawled on his back on the forest floor with his shirt soaked in blood. He was gasping for breath, his face ashen, his eyes closed. A woman she didn't recognize tore his shirt open while Ellie slapped an oxygen mask over his face.

Fiona must have asked what happened, though she didn't remember speaking, because Hal said, "He took a bullet to the chest."

She sank down beside him, clutching at his hand. It lay limp and cold in her grasp. Her friend was dying, and there was nothing she could do but hold his hand and watch…

Her snow leopard growled, jolting Fiona back to reality.

Your packmate survived, hissed the big cat. *And you will not get shot. We are too quick and clever for that.*

Right, Fiona replied, forcing herself to keep calm. *And now I know which producer is in with organized crime, so mission accomplished. Sort of.*

The burly man had said, "We're on to you," but he hadn't said who he thought she was. She'd constructed her cover identity well. Mr. Moore had probably found her in his office and called whoever his organized crime contact was—probably the same person who had arranged to have his desk booby trapped—and that person had sent in the hit men. Probably all they knew about her was that she carried a concealed weapon and had tried to break into the producer's desk.

"Please don't hurt me," she begged. "I'm sorry I tried to steal from you! But I didn't get any of your money. You can search me."

The hit men looked unconvinced. But Mr. Moore shot her a confused look, then asked the burly man, "She was after money, not information? Kurson, should we call the cops?"

"Shut up," said Kurson. "You've already said too much. And no, we're not calling the fucking cops. First, we find out for sure who she is and what she wanted. Then…" He glanced down at Fiona. "Then we decide what to do with her."

Then you kill me, she thought, chilled.

Fiona had seen his face, and Mr. Moore had given away his name. Even if she did convince them she was a thief, they wouldn't turn her over to the police. They wouldn't want law enforcement poking around their business, and the police would get very suspicious if she told them about the booby-trapped desk with its drugged needle. Not to mention that rather than calling 911 immediately, they'd tied her up and held her at gunpoint while debating what to do with her.

Fiona switched tactics, though she was rapidly losing faith in the possibility of talking her way out of this. She dropped the frightened expression, and said, "I'm with the FBI. If you take off right now, you have a chance to run for the border before my team breaks down the door. If you shoot me, they'll track you down no matter where you are."

She looked straight at Mr. Moore. "That goes for you too. It doesn't matter that you didn't personally pull the trigger. If they kill me, you just conspired to murder a federal agent. That's a death penalty offense."

The producer went white. Turning to Kurson, he said, "What do we do? I don't want to run for the border! Maybe we can make some kind of deal…"

Without taking his cold gaze from Fiona, Kurson replied, "What *you* do is leave this room. You called us in. We'll take it from here."

Mr. Moore turned around and began to hurry out.

Fiona called after him, "Leave now, and it's still conspi—"

Kurson kicked her in the ribs. "Shut up."

The door slammed, leaving her alone with the three men.

Shift now and take my chances? Fiona wondered. *Or wait it out?*

They obviously weren't going to kill her just yet—not without interrogating her to find out who she was and why she'd been spying on Mr. Moore. If she could play out the interrogation long enough, she'd miss her daily check-in with Protection, Inc., and her team would realize she was in trouble.

A cold finger of anxiety traced down her spine at the thought of exactly how they might interrogate her. Even an hour or so might feel like a very, very long time.

Biting her lip, she thought, *I'll wait. At least long enough for them to decide there's nothing I can do to them while I'm tied up, and stop aiming their guns right at my head.*

Kurson snapped his fingers. "Let's take her now."

Fiona kept her face expressionless, but inwardly she readied herself. If they were going to transport her somewhere to question more easily, she should have a better chance to jump them along the way. All else aside, one of them would have to drive. If she was really lucky, they'd stick her in the trunk. She imagined them telling their boss that the trunk had suddenly burst open en route, leaving them with no captive and no explanation other than that maybe she'd been carried off by the huge white leopard they'd seen running away, and had to suppress a smile.

One of the hit men stepped forward and knelt beside her. She had a split second to see the needle in his hand before he stuck it in her shoulder.

This is just not my day, she thought as everything went black.

CHAPTER SEVENTEEN

Grace

Grace was doing the job she loved, working on a play that could be a smash hit and make her career, with the man she loved standing at her side. They were almost all the way through the play, nothing serious had gone wrong, and the audience seemed to be loving it. The flying sequences had gone smoothly and looked great, with Paris and Brady floating through the air against a starry outer space backdrop. Grace even had a beautiful bouquet of roses wafting their sweet scent throughout the booth. She'd never been happier in her life.

And then Brady took his first bite of homemade, honey-sweetened, raspberry-flavored Mars jello. For once, he didn't pull a face. She didn't know if it was because props had finally gotten it flavored to his satisfaction, or whether he'd obeyed her order to act as if he enjoyed it no matter what, or if the fact that he finally had a real audience meant that he was going to buckle down and do his job. But whatever the reason, he was chewing it like it was the best thing he'd ever eaten.

"Finally," Grace muttered.

Brady kept on chewing.

And chewing.

And chewing.

"What the hell is he up to?" Grace muttered to Rafa, clicking off her microphone so her words wouldn't be transmitted to everyone on headset backstage. "It's jello! He's chewing it like it's bubblegum."

"Could it have come out too tough?" Rafa asked.

"Can't be. He dug into it with a spoon."

Brady's expression became increasingly desperate as he kept chewing. Finally, he spat the mouthful out on to the plate and ad-libbed, "That stuff's never going to replace McDonald's."

The audience burst out laughing.

Irritated, Grace clicked her microphone back on and said, "Carl, put Brady on headset when he gets backstage. Tell him we need to talk about the jello. Stage crew, stand by for scene change. Stand by for a blackout."

Brady spoke his final line. She blacked out the stage and said, "Scene change go." When Carl told her the scene change was complete, she brought the lights up for the next scene.

As the moons of Mars began to dance across the stage, Brady spoke into the microphone. "Grace! You've got to do something about the jello!"

"What was wrong with it this time?" As she spoke, she adjusted the spotlight to keep up with Melissa, who was dancing a little faster than usual.

"Too much gelatin," Brady said. "Instead of melting in my mouth, it just broke into smaller and smaller pieces. I ended up with a mouthful of wet sand! I had to spit it out, or I'd have choked on it."

"Sorry," Grace said, watching the stage. Now Melissa was dancing too slow. Grace slowed down the spotlight. "That does sound gross. Thanks for letting me know. I'll tell props. Stage crew, stand by for the scene change. Stand by for a blackout." She glanced at the backstage monitor. "Carl, it looks like someone spilled some water by the stage left entrance. Can you mop it fast, before someone slips in it?" She blacked out the stage lights. "Set change go."

As she brought up the lights and the next scene began, she split her attention between the stage and the backstage monitor. Backstage, Carl hurried toward the closet with the mops—the same one she and Rafa had once had amazing sex in.

Rafa clearly had the same thought, because he murmured, "Good times," and ran a finger across the back of her neck.

She shivered with a sudden wave of desire. Clicking off her microphone, she said, "Maybe after the show."

On the backstage monitor, Carl opened the closet and took out a mop. He started toward the puddle, then suddenly stopped by the stage door, which should have been closed but was standing ajar. His head jerked up at he stared at something outside. The monitor didn't cover that area, so Grace couldn't see what it was. But whatever it was, it had a strong effect on Carl. The mop fell from his hand. Then he bolted outside. The stage door swung shut behind him.

"What the hell…?" Grace muttered. "Rafa, did you see that?"

She glanced up at him. His face and body were radiating an alert readiness that she'd last seen when someone had shot at them. It scared the hell out of her.

"I saw it," Rafa said quietly. "The question is, what did Carl see? I better go find out."

Her stomach lurched with anxiety. "Be careful."

He lifted her hand and kissed it. "I'll come back to you. I promise."

Rafa was out of the booth and climbing down the ladder almost before she could blink. She went on running the lights and sound on autopilot, but she barely paid any attention to what was happening onstage. Instead, she watched Rafa on the backstage monitor as he stalked toward the door like a lion in human form. He looked strong and capable and confident, easily able to handle anything. Grace wanted to believe that he'd be fine no matter he faced.

I just wish I knew what Carl saw, she thought uneasily.

Rafa opened the door a crack, peered out, then opened it a little wider and stepped out.

The door closed behind him.

CHAPTER EIGHTEEN

Fiona

Fiona awoke standing up, with someone slapping her face. This time her memories flooded back immediately.

She was being held up by someone's firm grip on her shoulders. Her hands were still bound behind her back, but her ankles were no longer tied. Her hopes rose. It was looking like she now had a better chance to escape than she'd had in the office.

She opened her eyes, and her heart sank. She was unsurprised to see that Kurson was the one who was slapping her. But the man holding her up was new, and so were the men beside him. She was no longer facing three men with guns, but six. The odds, which had already been against her, were now even worse.

I shouldn't have waited, she thought, angry at herself. *I should have taken my chances and shifted in the office.*

Fiona was in a clearing in the middle of a dark, dense forest. She didn't recognize the exact location, but from the general look of the area, they'd driven her a bit north of Santa Martina. Those forests stretched out for miles. Nobody would hear her if she screamed. Her teammates would have no idea where she was and no way of tracking her there.

Fear gripped her at the thought that she might die there. Then it was replaced by an overwhelming loneliness. All but one of her teammates had found their mates, and surely Destiny would find hers soon. Only Fiona, whose ice-cold heart had ensured that she'd always live alone, would also die alone. She just hadn't thought it would be this soon.

You will survive, hissed her snow leopard.

Kurson had noticed her looking around. "Don't get any ideas about running. We'll shoot you down in a second. This is a good place to dispose of a body."

It is also a good place for a snow leopard, hissed her inner cat.

It was true. If she shifted—and she had no other choice, now—she could leap into the trees and vanish into the foliage. From there, she'd have the advantage, and could either escape or stalk her kidnappers. She just had to find the best opportunity to do it without getting shot first. How she'd engineer that, she didn't know. But it never hurt to poke at people to see what made them tick.

She got her feet under her, then jeered, "It takes six of you to kidnap one woman? I had no idea I was that scary."

She saw anger flicker in the eyes of the man who still gripped her shoulders, and felt his fingers tense.

But Kurson said evenly, "You carried two military-grade concealed weapons, and you claim to be a federal agent with a team backing you up. I'd say we're taking reasonable precautions."

Fiona looked him in the eyes. "I was under surveillance. My team is on their way right now. Only six of you? Should've brought twenty."

"Actually, there's seven," said a new voice.

A strange man stepped out of the shadows. While the kidnapper holding her shoulders didn't release her, she felt him give a start. The other four spun around, bringing their guns to bear on him. Only Kurson kept his gun trained on her.

Now! Fiona thought, and tensed to shift.

Cold steel jammed into her forehead. She froze. Kurson had the barrel of his gun pressed to her head.

"Stop!" Kurson barked. "Whatever you were about to do, I can put a bullet in your head faster than you can do it."

Fiona was so angry and frustrated that she nearly shifted anyway. But she forced her snarling snow leopard down. Kurson was right. There was no point throwing her life away.

"Easy," said the stranger. He was tall and lean, with black hair and dark eyes and handsome, angular features. His empty hands were raised in the air, but his voice was perfectly calm. "I'm with you."

"The hell you are," snapped one of the kidnappers. "I've never seen you before."

"*I've* never seen *you* before," the stranger pointed out. "But I'm not questioning who *you* work for. Mr. Abrams sent me."

All the kidnappers seemed to relax a little at that, though their guns didn't budge.

Ah-ha, Fiona thought. *So* that's *who's behind the whole thing.*

Like Wallace Nagle, whom Ellie had put behind bars, Mr. Abrams was known to be an organized crime boss. But, as had also been the case with Nagle, knowing was one thing and proving was another. The Santa Martina police had been trying to get charges to stick on Abrams for a long time, but it was difficult when witnesses were too intimidated to cooperate.

"I'm an interrogation specialist," the stranger went on. His tone was even more frightening than his words—not sadistic, but cold as ice. As if he was dead inside. And a man who felt nothing might do anything.

That seemed to convince Kurson. "Fine. Have at her. We're staying, though."

"Yes, do. I'll need you afterward. I didn't bring a shovel." With those unnerving words, delivered in the same flat tone, the stranger stepped toward her. He moved with an oddly familiar predatory grace, like a stalking cat.

Fiona knew she should be frightened at his approach, but instead she felt a strange mixture of curiosity and anticipation. He reminded her of someone…

Your packmate, hissed her snow leopard.

That was it: the stranger moved with something like Shane's coiled power. He'd even emerged from shadows, though when Shane did that, he gave the impression of materializing from thin air, while this man had simply seemed to be well-concealed.

He stopped in front of her. This close, she could see that his eyes were black as engine oil, so dark that she couldn't distinguish iris from pupil. The instant their gazes locked, a jolt went through her body, like she'd stuck her finger in a light socket.

The man gave a start, almost as if he'd felt it too.

Her snow leopard made a sound Fiona had never heard before, a low rumble halfway between a growl and a purr.

What was that? Fiona asked, uncertain even to herself whether she meant the jolt she'd felt or her snow leopard's reaction.

I… I don't know. Her inner cat seemed puzzled. *There is something about him… Something strange.*

And that in itself was strange. Her snow leopard was never confused or hesitant, even when she probably should be. The big cat had no understanding of ambiguity or gray areas. Why was she perplexed by this man?

The stranger stood in front of her, looking her over silently. Fiona wished she could read his expression, but his eyes were black mirrors, reflecting everything and giving away nothing. She needed to be able to understand him if she had a chance of defeating him. So she studied what she could of him.

He wore black jeans and a black leather jacket. She didn't see any weapons, but his clothes were baggy enough to conceal anything. Though maybe that wasn't why they were loosely fitted. Now that he was closer, she could see that his cheekbones and collarbones jutted harshly, as if he'd lost too much weight. His skin was very pale, almost translucent, and the shadows beneath his eyes were dark as bruises. A network of faint lines traced across his face, though otherwise he didn't look any older than she was.

Shane had looked like that in the hospital, when he'd just gotten out of surgery.

Maybe this guy's just recovered from an injury, she thought. *Or an illness.*

He has not recovered, hissed her snow leopard unexpectedly. *Whatever is wrong with him is not over.*

How can you tell? Fiona asked. *He doesn't move like he's weak or in pain.*

Her snow leopard gave a frustrated snort. *I don't know.*

Fiona believed the big cat, but even so, she didn't think he would be easy to fight. Not a man who moved like Shane.

The stranger turned his head to the men holding her. "Can I have some room to work?"

"Yeah." Kurson stepped away, to Fiona's relief. Not that the threat of being tortured was any better than the threat of being shot, but she was glad to have the gun barrel off her forehead. The man holding her shoulders also moved away.

She let her field of vision widen, so she could see what all the gangsters were doing without letting them see she was checking them out. They had their guns ready, but not aimed directly at her; the stranger was standing too close for them to be able to easily shoot her without hitting him. If she had her hands free, she could use him as a human shield. If she shifted, though, she'd be much bigger than him, and they could hit her easily. Still, this might be her best chance…

Wait, hissed her snow leopard.

That was strange too. Normally her snow leopard was the one urging her to leap into action, and Fiona was the one holding back.

The stranger laid one hand on her shoulder and reached behind her with his other hand to grasp her bound wrists. Another odd shock went through her at his touch, and she couldn't repress a start.

The stranger seemed to have felt it too: his hands had closed convulsively over her shoulder and wrists, then relaxed.

What the hell is going on?

He backed her up, putting his body between her and the other men. She could feel the heat of his body and smell his clean masculine scent.

He's placed himself perfectly to block the gangsters' view of both our faces, she realized. *If I'd done that, it would've been on purpose, so we could—*

In the barest whisper of sound, he murmured, "I'm on your side. If I give you a gun, can you shoot?"

A multitude of doubts and questions leaped into her mind—*Is this a trick? Is he an undercover cop? Is he a criminal using me to take out the competition, and he'll kill me once he's done with them?*—but she pushed them aside. Going along with him couldn't possibly be worse than not going along.

And though she had absolutely no reason to trust him, she did.

Fiona nodded.

"You a lefty?" he whispered.

She gave the tiniest shake of her head.

"Hit your head," he murmured.

He shoved her against a tree. Fiona let her head snap back and gave a cry of pain. A few malicious laughs arose from the watching gangsters. The distraction had worked.

The stranger bent over her, as if menacing her, and whispered, "I'm going to cut the cords and pass you a gun. Then I'll step to your left.

You take the three on the right. I'll take the three on the left. Got it?"

"Got it," she breathed.

Behind her back, his wrist twisted against hers. She felt the cold touch of metal as he sliced the cords that bound her, holding them so they wouldn't fall. Then he pushed the knife into her left hand and a very small pistol into her right. He waited until she'd gotten a good grip on them both. Then he moved smoothly to her left.

Now! Her snow leopard's snarl seemed as loud as the gunshots already sounding from her left as Fiona whipped up her gun hand and fired.

Gunshots echoed through the forest.

Then silence.

As fast as the battle had begun, it was over. Six men lay crumpled on the forest floor. They'd been taken so completely by surprise, she didn't think they'd had time to fire a single shot.

She and the stranger moved quickly to check the gangsters, and to disarm and tie up the ones who were only wounded. Then Fiona beckoned him across the clearing, where they could speak quietly without being overheard.

"Who—" The question died on her lips as she saw that the gangsters had gotten off at least one shot, after all. Blood was trickling out of the stranger's left jacket sleeve and on to the back of his gun hand.

Irrelevantly, she thought, *No wonder he asked if I was left-handed. He's used to the world not being made for him.*

"You're hit," she said.

"I am?" He sounded no more than mildly curious as he glanced down at himself. "Oh."

"Don't you feel it?"

He shook his head.

Fiona was alarmed. Not feeling pain might be because of an adrenaline rush, or it might mean he'd been so badly wounded that he'd already gone into shock, and would collapse at any moment. "Take off your jacket."

"It's all right. I'll take a look later."

He sounded so bizarrely unconcerned that he'd been *shot* that it made her worry even more. She ordered, "Take off your jacket, or I'll take it off for you!"

His eyebrows arched in something like amusement. "Don't trouble yourself."

He slipped off his jacket. The bullet had dug a gouge into his upper arm, but to her relief, it didn't look serious.

He glanced at the wound, then replaced his gun in its shoulder holster, which was strapped over a white T-shirt. Without the jacket to conceal his body, she could see that though he had enough muscle to look strong, he seemed too thin for his frame.

"Let me help you bandage that," she said. "I can rip up some clothes—"

"It's fine." He pulled his jacket back on. "I have to get going."

"Who are you? An undercover cop? FBI?"

He shook his head. "Just a passerby."

That was ridiculous, obviously, but if he was law enforcement, he should have said so. She wondered if he was a criminal after all—maybe even one of Abrams' gang, just like he'd said, having a crisis of conscience. "If this is on your way, you're on a hell of a long walk. Why did you help me?"

He shrugged. "I thought you were someone else."

"Do I look like her?"

His lips twitched into something resembling a smile, but there wasn't much humor in it. "Hardly. He's a guy."

The more he said, the more at sea Fiona felt. "Can you please just tell me what's going on?"

He was silent, studying her with his strange black eyes, then said, "We'll never see each other again, so I guess it doesn't matter. I thought a friend of mine was in danger, so I came to rescue him. He wasn't here, but you were. I spied on those gangsters and overheard them say their boss's name—and what they were going to do to you."

Fiona made a face. "Concluding with shovels, huh?"

"Yeah. You obviously needed a hand, so I gave you one. That's all."

"All? You saved my life." Fiona paused, frustrated. She wanted to give him something in return—help *him* in exchange, even in some tiny token way—but he obviously wanted nothing more than to get out of there. Since it was all she could do, she said, "Thank you."

"You're welcome. Listen, if you want to return the favor, don't tell anyone I helped you out. Don't tell anyone I *exist.* You're obviously capable of taking out six of those thugs, so just say you did."

"What about what the thugs say?"

"Tell them not to mention me, either. I'm sure you're capable of being persuasive, too." For the first time since he'd slipped her the gun, he reached out and touched her. There was no shock this time, just the pressure of his fingers on her shoulder, strong and warm. "Don't even tell whoever you normally tell your secrets to. Keep this one to yourself. Promise?"

He's on the run, she thought. *So is he a criminal? Or just a man in deep, deep trouble?*

He sounded terribly tired. Not just physically, which made sense after a gunfight, but weary down to the heart and soul. Like he was living a life that was eating away at him and had been for a very long time, but he didn't know how to stop.

Or maybe Fiona was just projecting that on him because once upon a time, she'd been there herself.

"I promise," she said. It seemed like the least that she could do. Though maybe there *was* something else she could help with. "Hey, what made you think they were doing something to your friend? Is he in trouble with them? Could they be holding him somewhere else?"

"No. He's fine. I know that now. I… I was wrong. I was wrong before, too. I…" He trailed off into a deep sigh. Very quietly, as if he wasn't even talking to her, he said, "Something's wrong with me."

Blood was dripping from his fingertips to the grass, but he still made no move to staunch the bleeding. Fiona began to rethink how badly injured he was. His weary tone, his pallor, the things he was saying, and the way he was behaving all made her wonder if either his wound was more serious than it had looked, or if he had another one that he didn't feel and she hadn't seen.

"I think so too," she said. "Let me take you to a hospital."

Instantly, he backed away, all the way up to the shadowy edge of the woods. "No. I'm fine."

Could he be a shifter, afraid to go to a hospital in case the doctors would notice that he was healing too quickly? Or, more likely, he just had an outstanding warrant. "I could take you to a doctor I know. A *discreet* doctor."

"I don't like doctors." From his tone, that was the understatement of the year. He went on, "You're in law enforcement, right? Go back to the city. Get the police or FBI or whoever you're with to clean up. The gangsters' cars are that way." He pointed.

Automatically, she turned to look. When she turned back, he was gone.

Catch him, hissed her snow leopard, but Fiona didn't need any encouragement.

"Wait!" She ran into the woods. "Wait…"

But he was nowhere to be seen. He'd vanished as easily as he'd appeared.

She wished he hadn't run away. She'd wanted to help him, and now she couldn't. He'd saved her life, and she'd barely even thanked him. She didn't even know his name.

She wished, too, that he hadn't made her promise not to tell *anyone* about him. Now she couldn't even tell Hal or Shane or Destiny.

Well, Fiona had so many secrets, what did one more matter? Anyway, she'd never see him again.

That knowledge made an odd pang go through her heart. But she shrugged it off. The important thing was that she'd found out who was behind the attacks on *Mars: The Musical.* Now she could keep Rafa and his mate safe.

Fiona returned to the wounded gangsters. Kurson gave her a furious glare as she crouched down beside him and slipped his car keys out of his pocket. To her annoyance, he didn't have a cell phone. Neither did any of the other gangsters.

"Nobody knows I'm here," Fiona said. "You don't even know who I am, so neither does your boss. So I've got two options. I could finish you off, and no one would ever know it was me. Or I could drive into town, get a phone, and call an ambulance. You'd all go to jail, but you'd survive. Up to you."

Kurson shot her a murderous glare, but he was helpless. Sullenly, he said, "What do you want?"

"Just two things. First, don't mention that guy who helped me. As far as you're concerned, I'm the only one who was ever here." She turned to stare at the rest of the gangsters. "Got it?"

"Yeah, fine," said Kurson. The other gangsters nodded. That part was obviously no skin off their teeth.

"Second thing. Who's sabotaging *Mars: The Musical?*"

Kurson scowled. Fiona kept her expression blank, but she was relieved to see that he obviously knew. That had been a gamble; the hit man could have just as easily have had no idea.

"What'll it be?" Fiona prompted. "Ambulance? Or shallow grave?"

"This guy Mr. Abrams hired special for the job. An undercover specialist. Like you. Only better. *He* didn't get caught." Kurson gave a nasty snicker.

"Sure he did," Fiona retorted. "I caught him just now. What's his name?"

"Jason Lindstrom."

"There's nobody by that name on the show."

"That's because he stole the identity of some theatre guy who's working in France right now."

"Who's that?" Fiona demanded.

"Carl…" Kurson shrugged. "I forget. Carl something."

That was all Fiona needed to know. She jumped up, car keys in hand.

With a sneer, Kurson added, "Too late. That show is already over. Permanently."

Cold fear crept up Fiona's spine. "What do you mean?"

"I guess you know Mr. Abrams hired someone else to take a shot at the stage manager a while back. Long distance assassination isn't Lindstrom's style. He likes to work close up, but Mr. Abrams thought that was too risky. Anyway, it didn't work. Some bodyguard protected her. So Mr. Abrams asked Lindstrom if he could work double duty and finish the job."

Kurson laughed again, even more nastily. "Mr. Abrams told him to lay off the sabotage. Told him to wait till opening night, when everyone would have figured he'd given up, and finish the job. It's opening night right now, so the stage manager's already dead. And if that bodyguard got in the way, so is he."

Fiona spun around and bolted in the direction the stranger had pointed. Sure enough, a couple cars were parked on a rough dirt road. Fiona unlocked one with the keys she'd taken from Kurson. She jumped in and stepped on the gas, praying she wasn't too late.

CHAPTER NINETEEN

Grace

The moments ticked away, and Rafa didn't return. Grace kept on running the lights and sound and set changes. She also talked a stagehand through taking over Carl's jobs, since Carl hadn't returned either. But though she kept her voice calm, her anxiety grew. What the hell was going on?

She debated sending a stagehand to go outside and report back to her. But if something dangerous was going on, she didn't want to send some innocent person straight into it. At best, they'd be at risk themselves; at worst, they'd also endanger Rafa further by sticking him with another person he'd have to protect. And if she went after him herself, she'd do the exact same thing.

If only she could reach Rafa over her headset...

I'm an idiot, Grace thought. *Who needs headsets? We have cell phones.*

She snatched her cell phone out of her purse. As she didn't want to distract him if he was in the middle of a fight or sneaking up on someone or who knows what, she texted instead of calling.

What is going on? Do you need help?

A sudden buzz almost made her leap out of her seat. She whipped around. It came from the pocket of the jacket Rafa had left draped over a chair. Grace leaned over and pulled out Rafa's cell phone.

Goddammit.

Maybe she should call the police, just in case. Given the sniper attack, they'd undoubtedly take the call seriously. Then she got a better idea. She hit a button to bring up the "Mars sunset" effect, told the stagehands to put in the sunset backdrop, and pulled up the contact list on Rafa's phone. She'd call his teammates and get them to check on him.

As she was about to dial Hal's number, she saw movement on the backstage monitor. The stage door opened. Carl hurried in, glanced up toward the camera, and held out his hands in a "hold on" gesture. Then he pointed to the ladder: he was coming up.

He didn't look scared or upset, so she was reassured that nothing terrible had happened. Perplexed, Grace put down Rafa's phone. She'd better get the report from Carl before she called anyone. It was odd that he hadn't just picked up a headset and told her whatever he had to say. But as she watched him climbing the ladder, it occurred to her that anyone could overhear everything spoken on headset. Maybe Rafa had given him a private message for her.

Carl climbed into the booth and glanced down at the stage. A scene was about to end, and there was a thirty-second blackout before the next scene started. It was the climax of the play, when Brady and Paris climbed into their jerry-rigged escape rocket, and was meant to build suspense to an almost unbearable degree. Grace could testify that even though she knew they made it safely back to Earth, she always felt an irrational anxiety during that long wait. Thirty seconds in a blackout, in dead silence, felt like an eternity.

Carl gestured to her to go ahead.

"Stand by for blackout. Silence backstage during the blackout, everyone," Grace said. "Absolutely no speaking, walking, or even touching anything till I say it's over."

She hit the button, plunging the stage into darkness, then turned off her mike to speak to Carl. "What's going on? Is Rafa okay?"

"He's fine," Carl assured her.

She was immensely relieved. "Where is he? What's going on?"

"I'll show you." Carl beckoned to her to step away from the board.

Grace took a quick glance at her watch. She still had twenty seconds before she needed to bring up the lights, so she took off her headset and stepped toward him. "What is—"

A glint of light shone at the end of Carl's right sleeve, as if it was concealing a watch. But Carl was right-handed; he wore his watch on his left wrist. He was wearing it now. And she'd never seen him wear a bracelet…

Grace leaped back at the exact instant that Carl whipped up his right hand. With a soft and terrifying click, the concealed switchblade flicked out and slashed through the air where her throat had been a second ago.

Terrified, she scrambled backward. Her back thudded into the wall. She was trapped. The booth was so small, Carl was blocking both the exit and her access to her headset. She couldn't escape, and she couldn't call backstage for help. She couldn't call for help, period; the booth was soundproofed.

Carl gave a malicious chuckle as he watched her frantically looking around.

Stalling for time, she said, "It was you all along, wasn't it? You were doing everything when you went for coffee!"

"You got it. Well, I set up the flying accident when I went for coffee, but I executed it with a remote control I had in my pocket. I couldn't have everything happen when I was out of sight, or you'd have noticed. You're pretty observant."

"But what did you do to Rafa?"

"Oh, nothing much. Just spilled a little water to get your attention, then lured him into one of my little booby traps. Well, I shouldn't say *little*. I rigged a brick wall to collapse on top of him." Carl smiled. "It looked like he broke his leg, so he won't be going anywhere. I'll finish him off when I'm done with you."

Grace was torn between relief and fear. Rafa was alive. And she didn't think Carl would have an easy time with him, broken leg notwithstanding. But he wouldn't be coming to save her.

"But why? Why are you doing any of this?" As Grace spoke, drawing his attention, she let one of her hands drift behind her back, feeling around for something she could use as a weapon. But all she felt was the smooth wall.

Carl shrugged. "Money."

"I can pay you more," Grace said desperately. "Rafa's rich."

"As if he'd pay me off after you told him I threatened you. I know his type. Brave. Protective. *Honorable.*" The final word came out in a contemptuous sneer. "Okay, enough stalling. Your time's up."

He took a step toward her. Light flashed off the razor-sharp blade.

"RAFA!" Grace yelled.

Carl gave a nasty laugh. "Your boyfriend's not coming for you. He's got a broken leg, and this booth is only accessible by a vertical ladder."

"So what," growled Rafa.

Carl whipped around, his switchblade upraised. Rafa loomed behind him, an avenging fury in the shape of a man. His clothes were torn and dirty, blood was dripping from his hair, and he stood with all his weight balanced on one leg and one hand braced on the wall. He was the most beautiful sight Grace had ever seen.

Carl lunged at him, his switchblade a steel blur in the air. Rafa's free hand swung up, just as fast, and blocked the blow. But Carl aimed a vicious kick at his injured leg. Rafa fell with a grunt of pain, but took Carl down with him. The men struggled on the floor, fighting hard.

Grace smashed the heavy black vase of roses over Carl's head.

Carl went limp. Rafa shoved him to the side, then rolled him unceremoniously on to his stomach, yanked his hands behind his back, and handcuffed him.

Grace dropped to her knees beside Rafa. "You saved my life!"

Wincing, Rafa sat up and ruffled her hair. "Pretty sure you saved your own life. Good move with the vase."

"He would've killed me if you hadn't shown up," Grace said, shuddering. "Anyway, you gave me the vase."

"From now on, I'm only giving you romantic gifts that can double as improvised weapons," Rafa said, smiling. Then he frowned, glancing up. "Hey, is the show still going on? Shouldn't you be on headset?"

She looked up. The stage was still in darkness. The thirty-second blackout had lasted… three minutes? Five? "Yeah, but you're hurt! I have to call an ambulance."

Ignoring her headset, she picked up Rafa's cell phone and started to dial 911.

"No!" He snatched it out of her hand. "I can't go to a hospital, remember? I'll call my team. They'll take me to a doctor. You get back to work. I know how much this show means to you."

Reluctantly, she lifted her headset. Before she put it on, she took one last look at Rafa. His brown skin had paled and taken on a grayish tinge. Rather than making the call, he was sitting with his head down and his hand pressed to his forehead.

"Rafa!"

"I'm fine," he said, but his voice was alarmingly weak. "Just a little dizzy."

She grabbed the phone back. "Forget the play. This is your *life.*"

Grace dialed Hal. To her dismay, it went to voicemail. She left a hurried message, then called Destiny. That also went to voicemail. Frustrated, she left another message, then turned to ask Rafa who he thought was most likely to pick up.

Rafa had gotten off the floor and seated himself in her chair. He was wearing her headset and talking into it. The stage was no longer dark, but correctly set up and lit for the final scene, with the astronauts back on Earth. Paris and Brady were onstage, singing about the wonder of space exploration and the power of love. When they sang the final notes, Rafa hit a button on the light board, blacking out the stage.

"Stand by for curtain call," he said. "Tell me when everyone's in place. Okay, I'm bringing the lights up."

As Grace watched incredulously, he hit another button, bringing up the curtain call lights. The actors took their bows. Thunderous applause rose up from the audience. Grace peered out the window. They were getting a standing ovation.

"How'd you learn to do my job?" she asked, bewildered.

Rafa smiled. "I like watching you work, remember?"

He passed over the headset. Grace executed the final cues of the evening, blacking out the stage and bringing up the lights on the audience, then took off her headset and held up his cell phone. "I couldn't reach Hal and Destiny, so I had to leave messages. Who should I try calling next?"

Rafa peered at the backstage monitor. "Nobody. You already got through. Look, Hal or Destiny called in the cavalry."

Grace looked over his shoulder. Sure enough, his entire team was hurrying toward the ladder, with Fiona at the forefront. All of them were dressed for a night out, in suits or fancy dresses, except for Fiona, who was in a torn and dirty business suit.

"I don't get it," Grace said. "I just called them a minute ago. They couldn't possibly have gotten here so soon."

Rafa shrugged, then winced. "Can you tell them I'm okay? Otherwise they'll all come swarming up here, and they won't fit."

Grace went over to the ladder and yelled down, "Hey! Rafa said to tell you he's all right, and not to all climb up at once. You won't fit. He broke his leg, so you'll have to help him get down somehow. Oh, and Carl turned out to be a bad guy. He's here too, handcuffed and out cold. I guess we could just throw him down."

The team looked at each other, and then Hal called, "Give us a second to figure this out. Then I'll send up a couple people."

Grace returned to Rafa. He was still sitting in her chair, his leg stuck out awkwardly in front of him.

She put her arm around his shoulders. "Hey, thanks for doing my job for me."

"Thanks for doing *my* job for *me,*" Rafa returned.

Catalina climbed into the booth, followed by Shane and Fiona. They stepped over Carl, except for Fiona, whose foot came down hard on his outstretched hand. Grace was pretty sure that was no accident.

Grace squeezed aside to let the paramedics get to Rafa. They quickly checked him over.

"How is he?" Grace asked.

"He's fine," Catalina reassured her. "His leg's broken, but that'll heal in a couple weeks. The rest is just cuts and bruises."

"Are you sure?" Grace said anxiously. "He's so pale, and he said he felt dizzy…"

"That's just from pain." Shane filled a syringe and stuck a needle in Rafa's arm. "Watch, his color will come back. Just give this a couple minutes to work."

"I'm fine," Rafa promised her. "Shane's right. My leg just hurts like hell. Especially since I had to climb a ladder with it, and then Carl kicked me in it."

Fiona looked thoughtfully down at Carl, who was still out like a light. Grace suspected that he was going to get "accidentally" stepped on again on her way out.

While Catalina and Shane splinted Rafa's leg, Fiona gave them a quick rundown on what she'd learned while undercover.

"A crime boss named Abrams is behind the entire plot," Fiona explained. "He was an investor in *My Fair Lady*, and he wasn't going to let it sink or swim on its own merits." She gave Carl a hard nudge in the ribs with her foot. "He hired the sniper, and this guy too. His name isn't really Carl, it's Jason Lindstrom. The real Carl is working on a play in France."

"But how did you all get here so fast?" Rafa asked.

Catalina laughed. "We were already here! Everyone but Fiona had come to see the show. We were going to surprise you guys, so we came in at the last minute and sat in the back."

"The police can collect Lindstrom here." Fiona gave him another hard prod with her foot. "I already gave them a heads-up to arrest Abrams, one of the *My Fair Lady* producers, and a bunch of gangsters—it's a long story. But you've got nothing to worry about any more, Grace. They're all going to jail."

Someone cleared their throat loudly. Grace turned to see Lubomir, standing on the ladder and looking into the booth, his eyes wide.

"Rafa, are you all right?" the director asked.

"I'm fine," Rafa replied. "I broke my leg, but… I'm fine."

As Shane had promised, he did look much better now that the pain-killer had taken effect. Grace's anxiety slipped away. He'd need some time to recover, but he was obviously going to. And he was equally obviously in good hands.

"And Carl?" Lubomir asked.

"Carl tried to kill me and Rafa," Grace said. "That's why we had a five-minute blackout. It won't happen again."

"The plot against *Mars* is over," Rafa assured the director. "We found out who was behind it, and they're all either under arrest or about to be."

"Well… Thank you!" Lubomir looked perplexed but relieved. "We're having a cast party on the stage. Come down and join us when you can."

He climbed down. A moment later, several police officers arrived at the theatre, then climbed up and hauled Carl down, then off to jail. Once that was done, Catalina and Shane helped Rafa down the ladder, followed by Fiona and Grace.

They were met onstage by the Protection, Inc. team, plus the cast, crew, and musicians of *Mars,* who were celebrating with champagne and confetti, cupcakes and roses.

"Rafa!" Paris exclaimed. "Are you all right? Lubomir said Carl tried to kill you...?"

"It's a long story." Rafa turned to Shane and Catalina. "Can I not be hauled back to the office immediately? If someone gets me a chair, I'll be fine, honestly. I don't want to miss the party."

Shane and Catalina glanced at each other.

"One hour," Catalina said firmly. "It'll take the doctor longer than that to get to the office. And then we take you to her. No arguments."

"And no alcohol," Shane added. "You can have your champagne some other day."

Grace fetched Rafa a space shuttle seat, then settled in another one beside him. Several members of the audience joined the party, including Raluca in an exquisite designer gown, Journey, bedecked in the most expensive-looking jewelry Grace had ever seen, and even Nick's friend Manuel in a suit borrowed from someone with broader shoulders and shorter legs.

Ellie was accompanied by a man she introduced as her twin brother Ethan, who had the same sandy hair, blue-green eyes, and snub nose. He was dressed in battered Marine fatigues, and apologetically said that he'd just flown in from Afghanistan and arrived as Ellie and Hal were leaving to see a play, and Ellie had grabbed him and hustled him off with them.

"So..." Rafa began, glancing from Ethan to Ellie. "Does he...?"

Ellie shook her head, smiling. "Didn't have time."

"What?" Ethan asked.

"I'm pregnant!" Ellie announced, loudly enough that the *Mars* people stopped talking to listen. "With twins!"

The emotion on Ethan's unguarded face was so raw that Grace had to look away lest it bring tears to her eyes too. Then Ethan grabbed his sister in a hug that lifted her off her feet. When he finally put her down, he swiped his arm across his eyes, then said, "That was worth coming home for. Do I get to name them?"

"You can *help* name them," Ellie replied. "Hal and I get a veto in case you try to name them something like Spike and Rambo."

"Only if they're boys," Ethan said. "If they're girls, they should be Spikette and Rambina."

Destiny poked him in the ribs. "Hey, weirdo. Long time no see."

"Did you miss me?" Ethan asked.

Destiny flipped back her braids in a show of unconcern. "Oh, well, not you specifically. It's just handy to have a Marine on call."

Brady tapped Grace on the shoulder. "About the jello…"

"Sorry, Brady," she said. "It'll never happen again. Maybe I can get Paris to make it for you next time."

He shook his head. "No, it's fine. I realize now that I just hate jello. But I talked to Lubomir, and he said the audience loved my McDonald's joke so much, we're going to keep it. From now on, I take one bite, make a face, and spit it out. So it doesn't matter how gross it is—I never have to swallow it again!"

Ruth ran in, beaming. "Guess who I was sitting next to?" Not waiting for a reply, she said, "The theatre critic! With his wife! Guess what I heard him say to her about the show?" Again without a pause, she went on, "He loved it! He said the music was catchy, the story was thrilling, and the five minutes in black was a daring and brilliant directorial choice that made him feel like he was there with the lost astronauts in the lonely void of outer space! He said the headline on his review would be *MARS: THE MARVELOUS!*"

The actors broke into cheers.

"He liked the five-minute blackout?" said Lubomir incredulously. "I wonder if I should keep it? Or at least extend it to sixty seconds…"

Only then did Ruth notice the splint on Rafa's leg. "What happened to you?!"

"I broke my leg," he replied.

Ruth's eyebrows shot up. "I'm not superstitious. But next time, I'm sticking with 'good luck.'"

Manuel came up to Grace and Rafa, looking very happy and very nervous. "Excuse me. Can you introduce me to—or, um, just point out the director to me?"

"I'm the director," said Lubomir.

"Oh!" Manuel stared at him. "Well… I wanted to tell you… Actually, I should probably tell Nick too…"

Nick came up. "What?"

Now a whole crowd was watching Manuel. Dividing his attention between Lubomir and Nick, he said, "Um, I'm in college. I have to declare a major soon, but I didn't know what I wanted to do. I'd been following Nick around to see if I might want to be a bodyguard, but it's not for me. But then I came to see this play—just because Nick was going, otherwise I never would have come, I've never seen a play before in my life—"

A giddy smile broke over his face. "And I was sitting there watching the scene where the astronauts are landing on Mars, and I thought, 'That's what I want to do for the rest of my life.'"

"Study Mars?" Ruth asked eagerly. "Or be an astronaut?"

Manuel shook his head. "Do theatre! I want to create something like this show. I want to write musicals! Or maybe direct them. Or act. Or do the lights, I don't know, I just want to be a part of it all."

"Congratulations," Raluca said solemnly. "It is a very important thing, to know what you wish to do in life."

"Yeah, that's great," said Nick. He glanced at Lubomir. "He's here for a couple more days. Could someone show him around, maybe? Let him see how everything works?"

"Of course," Lubomir said. Looking from Grace to Paris to the conductor, he said, "Actually, I think we can do better than that. If you like, you can stay backstage for the next few performances, and follow a different person each night. I can tell you about directing, Paris can tell you about acting, perhaps you can sit beside Grace and see how stage management works…"

Manuel's big brown eyes lit up. "Oh, yes please!"

"Sure," said Grace. "And the theatre's completely safe now."

"Speaking of that," Lubomir said plaintively, "Can someone please explain exactly what happened?"

Everyone gathered round to listen as Rafa, Grace, Fiona, and Hal began to recount the story. When they got to Carl's attack in the booth, Rafa declared, "Grace saved my life."

"Actually, he saved mine," said Grace.

But she wasn't going to argue too hard. He'd looked after her, and he'd let her look after him. He'd not only saved her life, he'd saved her show. More importantly, he'd loved and understood her enough to remember what was important to her, and make sure she got it, no matter what it cost him. He'd even bought that heavy vase because he'd known she'd like it better than a conventionally pretty one—and the usual sort of vase would have been too delicate to knock Carl out.

He's not too good to be true, Grace thought contentedly as she stroked his hair. *And neither is our life together. It's good* and *true.*

She could trust in that.

EPILOGUE

Rafa

Rafa sat in the passenger seat and watched Grace drive. He couldn't wait to get the cast off his leg so he could drive again, not to mention walk without crutches again, but there were compensations. Grace had never owned a car that wasn't used and practical until he'd bought her a sleek black Ferrari for Christmas, and seeing her delight as she drove it was even more fun than driving it himself.

She looked more radiant and beautiful than ever, dressed to meet his family in an black silk dress with subtle black leather accents, and his other Christmas gift to her, a pair of silver earrings in the shape of tiny dangling spiders, in her ears. The wind from the open window sent her purple curls flying. He touched the butterfly tattoo behind her ear, and the words she lived by: *fly free.*

On the radio, "Jingle Bells" came on for the millionth time.

"How about something a little less overplayed?" Grace suggested.

Rafa switched channels until he came across a rundown of entertainment news. He stayed on that, figuring Grace would be interested. They listened to a report on the top ten movies, and then the announcer said, "And in theatre news, *My Fair Lady* announced its closing after a brief and troubled run which included the arrest of one of its producers and a secret financial backer on charges of sabotage, racketeering, and four counts of attempted murder. Meanwhile, *Mars: The Musical* continues to rule the box office. As of today, it has broken records for opening week ticket sales, and looks well on its way to becoming *Mars:*

The Moneymaker."

"Woo-hoo!" Grace cheered, pumping her fist. "We did it!"

"You did it," said Rafa.

The radio announcer continued, "And finally, the long-running hit *The Bottom of the Bottle* is in trouble. During a sold-out performance, the producer added twenty folding chairs in unsafe areas, causing an audience member to fall ten feet on to a concrete floor. Luckily, he was only bruised. But an eight thousand dollar bottle of Dom Perignon champagne, which he had intended to give his fiancée as an engagement present after the show, was smashed. He is now suing the producer, who is also under investigation for violating safety regulations. It may be that a broken bottle will spell ruin for the producer of *The Bottom of the Bottle.*"

"Merry Christmas," Rafa remarked. "It's your present."

Grace grinned at him. "I'd say it's too good to be true, but I don't say that any more."

She pulled up in front of his parents' house, then walked around and opened the car door for him. Rafa extracted himself and his crutch from the car, saying, "One more week, and I can open yours for you again."

"What, and hog all the fun?" Grace protested. "One more week, and we'll start taking turns."

They walked to the front door together, but he paused to see if Grace looked worried before he opened it. He was glad to see that she didn't.

As if she'd read his mind, she said, "A month ago I'd have been nervous about meeting your parents. But that was before I got shot at, had my assistant try to murder me, had Shane try to scare the living daylights out of me, had Destiny lay the world's biggest guilt trip on me, and watched you turn into a lion. I think tonight's going to go just fine."

"I know it will," Rafa said.

He opened the door and escorted her inside. His family home was decorated for Christmas, with an enormous tree topped with a rearing lion. His parents came up to meet Grace, with his sisters, their mates, and assorted cousins, nephews, nieces, aunts, uncles, and grandparents crowding behind.

"Everybody, this is Grace Chang, the stage manager who saved my life," Rafa said. With so much pride and happiness that he felt like he might burst with it, he added, "She's my mate."

A dead silence fell as his entire family stared at them.

His mother broke it. "About time!"

And then everyone jumped in, introducing themselves and asking Grace about herself and offering her drinks and snacks.

"Are those *spiders?*" squeaked his littlest niece. "That's so cool!"

"Oh, I wish I'd known," Grace said. "I'd have gotten you a pair. Are your ears pierced?"

Her mother replied with a sigh, "I've been trying and trying to convince her—I've told her it only hurts for a second—but she just won't do it."

Her eyes gleaming, his niece said, "I'll get my ears pierced if Uncle Rafa's mate gets me silver spider earrings!"

"Done," Grace said instantly.

"You know, we despaired of Rafa ever finding his mate," his great-grandmother confided to her. "I'd thought for a while it would be this tall blonde girl he was friends with in high school—what was her name?"

"Paris Hale," Rafa said. "And it was never going to be her. She called me this morning to tell me she just got engaged."

His great-grandmother waved her wrinkled hand in an airy gesture. "How nice for her. Anyway, that Paris girl was very pretty, but too thin. But you! You have good wide hips for bearing babies and nice plump breasts for nursing them. I can tell from your body that you'll be very fertile!"

"Grandma, please don't say stuff like that." Rafa could feel a hot tide of blood rising in his face.

Ignoring him, his great-grandmother went on, "So when are you two going to have your first cubs?"

"Cubs?" Grace echoed. She shot Rafa a desperate look.

"Let me get my mate a drink." He grabbed Grace's arm and hustled her into the kitchen. Once they were alone, he said, "I'm so sorry about my great-grandma. I had no idea she was going to go on about fertility."

"That was definitely the most unusual compliment I've ever gotten," Grace said with a giggle. "Cubs are babies, right?"

"Right."

He suddenly realized that in all the time they'd spent together, they'd never talked about children. Grace had been so excited about Ellie's pregnancy, and had told so many funny stories about the kids she'd used to babysit that he'd just assumed they were on the same page about that. With a pang of worry, he said, "*Do* you want to have kids?"

"Oh, man, we never talked about that, did we?" Grace said. Now *she* looked worried. "Yeah, I do. Do you?"

"Yes," Rafa replied, hugely relieved. "I've always wanted to. I just thought it was never going to happen."

"Me too!" Grace exclaimed. "On both counts. I want to keep working, though. But I'm guessing your family would be happy to babysit."

"For my cubs? They'd be over the moon."

A polite throat-clearing made them both turn around. It was his mother, looking as pleased as if she'd just pulled down the world's biggest antelope. "I couldn't help overhearing your conversation."

Rafa knew perfectly well that she'd been eavesdropping, but he didn't contradict her.

"Of course we'd be delighted to babysit," his mother went on. Stepping closer to Grace, she said quietly, "I worry about my son. I know what a dangerous job he has. But I feel better about it now that he has you. He told me what you did for him even before he told me what you were to him. You may not be able to shift, but you're a true lioness. I trust you to protect him, just as I trust him to protect you."

Rafa could see how moved Grace was by his mother's words. So was he.

"Thank you, Mrs. Flores," Grace replied. "I'll do my best."

"So," his mother said briskly. "When *do* you plan to get pregnant?"

Rafa groaned. "Mom!"

It was late at night when they returned to the new apartment that they'd gotten on the basis that Grace's old apartment was too small and Rafa's old apartment was too "swinging bachelor pad."

Once the door closed behind them, Rafa and Grace looked at each other. They didn't need to speak to say what they wanted, but headed straight for the bedroom. Rafa sat down on the bed and leaned his crutch against the wall. Grace helped him take off his shoes and pants, then slipped off his coat and unbuttoned his shirt with teasing slowness, letting her fingers trail across his chest with each button she undid. She knelt on the bed so he could undress her in turn, loosening the ribbons on her dress and stripping off her slip, her lacy bra, her panties.

By the time they were both nude, he was on fire with desire. But after the first kiss, Grace broke off and jumped off the bed. "Wait!"

"Where are you going?" he asked.

"You'll see." She darted into the next room, then returned with a glass bowl filled to the brim with sweetly scented red rose petals. "We never did make love on a bed of rose petals. And I know you want to."

Rafa's heart was so full, he didn't know whether to laugh or cry. "You're the best mate ever."

"What's the point of being a stage manager if I can't stage manage a perfect romantic evening for my mate?" Grace replied.

He reached for her, but she slipped from his grasp with a teasing smile.

"Lights…" Grace turned a switch to dim the lights.

"Sound…" She clicked a remote. Romantic music began to play.

"Roses…" She shook a rain of scented petals on to the covers.

"Go!" Rafa finished, and drew his mate down to the bed.

A NOTE FROM ZOE CHANT

Thank you for reading *Leader Lion!* I hope you enjoyed it. The final book in the Protection, Inc. series, *Top Gun Tiger*, is coming soon!

If you enjoy *Protection, Inc,* I also write the *Werewolf Marines* series under the pen name of Lia Silver. Both series have hot romances, exciting action, emotional healing, brave heroines who stand up for their men, and strong heroes who protect their mates with their lives.

Please consider reviewing *Leader Lion*, even if you only write a line or two. I appreciate all reviews, whether positive or negative.

Curious about the mysterious man who rescued Fiona? Page down to read a special sneak preview of *Soldier Snow Leopard*!

The cover of *Leader Lion* was designed by Augusta Scarlett.

ZOE CHANT WRITING AS LIA SILVER

The *Werewolf Marines* series
Laura's Wolf
Prisoner
Partner

Standalone
Mated to the Meerkat

ZOE CHANT WRITING AS LAUREN ESKER

The *Shifter Agents* series
Handcuffed to the Bear
Guard Wolf
Dragon's Luck
Tiger in the Hot Zone

The *Ladies of the Pack* series
Keeping Her Pride

The *Warriors of Galatea* series
Metal Wolf

Standalone
Wolf in Sheep's Clothing

ZOE CHANT WRITING AS HELEN KEEBLE

Standalones
Fang Girl
No Angel

ZOE CHANT
COMPLETE BOOK LIST

All books are available through Amazon.com.
Check my website, zoechant.com, for my latest releases.

While series should ideally be read in order, all of my books are stand-alones with happily ever afters and no cliffhangers. This includes books within series.

BOOKS IN SERIES

Protection, Inc.
Book 1: *Bodyguard Bear*
Book 2: *Defender Dragon*
Book 3: *Protector Panther*
Book 4: *Warrior Wolf*
Book 5: *Leader Lion*
Book 6: *Soldier Snow Leopard*

Bears of Pinerock County
Book 1: *Sheriff Bear*
Book 2: *Bad Boy Bear*
Book 3: *Alpha Rancher Bear*
Book 4: *Mountain Guardian Bear*
Book 5: *Hired Bear*
Book 6: *A Pinerock Bear Christmas*

Bodyguard Shifters
Book 1: *Bearista*
Book 2: *Pet Rescue Panther*
Book 3: *Bear in a Book Shop*

Cedar Hill Lions
Book 1: *Lawman Lion*
Book 2: *Guardian Lion*
Book 3: *Rancher Lion*
Book 4: *Second Chance Lion*
Book 5: *Protector Lion*

Christmas Valley Shifters
Book 1: *The Christmas Dragon's Mate*
Book 2: *The Christmas Dragon's Heart*

Enforcer Bears
Book 1: *Bear Cop*
Book 2: *Hunter Bear*
Book 3: *Wedding Bear*
Book 4: *Fighter Bear*
Book 5: *Bear Guard*

Fire & Rescue Shifters
Book 1: *Firefighter Dragon*
Book 2: *Firefighter Pegasus*
Book 3: *Firefighter Griffin*
Book 4: *Firefighter Sea Dragon*
Book 5: *The Master Shark's Mate*
Book 6: *Firefighter Unicorn*
Book 7: *Firefighter Pegasus*

Glacier Leopards
Book 1: *The Snow Leopard's Mate*
Book 2: *The Snow Leopard's Baby*
Book 3: *The Snow Leopard's Home*
Book 4: *The Snow Leopard's Heart*

Gray's Hollow Dragon Shifters
Book 1: *The Billionaire Dragon Shifter's Mate*
Book 2: *Beauty and the Billionaire Dragon Shifter*
Book 3: *The Billionaire Dragon Shifter's Christmas*
Book 4: *Choosing the Billionaire Dragon Shifters*
Book 5: *The Billionaire Dragon Shifter's Baby*
Book 6: *The Billionaire Dragon Shifter Meets His Match*

Hollywood Shifters
Book 1: *Hollywood Bear*
Book 2: *Hollywood Dragon*
Book 3: *Hollywood Tiger*
Book 4: *A Hollywood Shifters' Christmas*

Honey for the Billionbear
Book 1: *Honey for the Billionbear*
Book 2: *Guarding His Honey*
Book 3: *The Bear and His Honey*

Ranch Romeos
Book 1: *Bear West*
Book 2: *The Billionaire Wolf Needs a Wife*

Rowland Lions
Book 1: *Lion's Hunt*
Book 2: *Lion's Mate*

Shifter Kingdom
Book 1: *Royal Guard Lion*
Book 2: *Royal Guard Tiger*

Shifter Suspense
Book 1: *Panther's Promise*
Book 2: *Saved by the Billionaire Lion Shifter*
Book 3: *Stealing the Snow Leopard's Heart*

Shifting Sands Resort
Book 1: *Tropical Tiger Spy*
Book 2: *Tropical Wounded Wolf*

Upson Downs
Book 1: *Target: Billionbear*
Book 2: *A Werewolf's Valentine*

NON-SERIES BOOKS

Bears

A Pair of Bears
Alpha Bear Detective
Bear Down
Bear Mechanic
Bear Watching
Bear With Me
Bearing Your Soul
Bearly There
Bought by the Billionbear
Country Star Bear
Dancing Bearfoot
Hero Bear
In the Billionbear's Den
Kodiak Moment
Private Eye Bear's Mate
The Bear Comes Home For Christmas
The Bear With No Name
The Bear's Christmas Bride
The Billionbear's Bride
The Easter Bunny's Bear
The Hawk and Her LumBEARjack

Big Cats

Alpha Lion
Joining the Jaguar

Loved by the Lion
Pursued by the Puma
Rescued by the Jaguar
Royal Guard Lion
The Billionaire Jaguar's Curvy Journalist
The Jaguar's Beach Bride
The Saber Tooth Tiger's Mate
Trusting the Tiger

Dragons

The Christmas Dragon's Mate
The Dragon Billionaire's Secret Mate
The Mountain Dragon's Curvy Mate
A Mate for the Christmas Dragon

Eagles

Wild Flight

Griffins

The Griffin's Mate
Ranger Griffin

Wolves

Alpha on the Run
Healing Her Wolf
Undercover Alpha
Wolf Home

SOLDIER SNOW LEOPARD

PROTECTION, INC. # 6

SNEAK PREVIEW

Justin

Justin Kovac sat in a car parked alongside a lonely country road, getting ready to track down his enemy.

The sky looked hard as steel, and was about the same color. The leafless trees seemed to claw at it with bony fingers. Hail rattled down and piled up on the dark earth.

When Justin's gaze drifted to the rear-view mirror, he saw a face fit for the colorless landscape: skin pale as the hailstones, eyes and hair black as winter ponds. Cheekbones like knives. A mouth that had forgotten how to smile.

He could barely see a trace of the man he'd once been. That man, whose buddies had called him Red, had laughed and joked his way through life. He'd loved his team and his life in the Air Force. He'd believed that he'd lay down his life to save his friends. Then he and his team had been kidnapped by the black ops agency called Apex. And he'd learned that being willing to give your life doesn't make it happen.

The brave men and women who'd been captured with him had died trying to save *him,* leaving him the sole survivor. And then there was nothing standing between him and Apex.

Apex had made him into a shifter. Given him special powers. And taken away everything that made him who he was. He'd lost his friends. His career. His honor. His integrity. His hope. His laughter. Even the color of his eyes.

He'd become Subject Seven, their lab rat. And their assassin.

The only thing Apex had been unable to take from him was his longing for freedom.

Now he had his freedom. And he had no idea what to do with it.

I have an idea, hissed his inner snow leopard. *We should hunt.*

"You're so literal." Justin spoke aloud. His breath clouded in the freezing air. "I meant that I don't know what to do with my entire life."

But his snow leopard was right. One Apex base had been destroyed when he'd broken loose, but he knew there was at least one remaining. He didn't know where it was, any more than he knew the current whereabouts of the surviving Apex agents from the base where he'd been imprisoned. But he meant to find out.

"Just one left." A streamer of mist fluttered from Justin's lips as he spoke. "Well, just one left that I can track with my power."

You must find them all, hissed his snow leopard. *Find them and kill them!*

"I'm working on it." As Justin reached up to push a lock of hair out of his eyes, his arm brushed against the cold metal of the door handle.

Instantly, he was hurled into a memory.

The metal of the lab table was icy against his bare skin. He was strapped down, with the usual array of sensors attached to his body.

Dr. Attanasio approached him with a syringe full of blue-green liquid.

"What's that?" Justin asked, doing his best to keep his voice steady.

"A little something I designed to make you stronger," the doctor said with pride.

"Why the straps?"

"You'll see," the doctor said, with a sadistic smile hovering at his lips. He lowered the syringe to Justin's arm.

The liquid burned in his veins. Justin gritted his teeth, waiting for the sensation to die down. But it didn't. Instead, the burning spread throughout his body, getting more painful by the second, until he felt like he'd been engulfed in flame.

Maybe the stuff increased his strength a little bit, but it didn't make him strong enough to break the straps, which had been designed to hold down shifters.

But even while he was screaming and struggling, unable to stop himself, he noticed when Dr. Attanasio came a little bit closer than he should have to replace a dislodged sensor. Justin's arms were strapped down, but he managed to stealthily move one finger to brush against the tiny bit of bare skin between the doctor's latex glove and the cuff of his white coat.

Dr. Attanasio never noticed. But Justin felt that sense of imprint, *impossible to describe but unmistakable, and knew he'd be able to find the doctor again, no matter where he hid.*

There was a strap over his chest. A strap across his waist. Cold metal against his arm. He was trapped.

His snow leopard's shriek of terror and rage rose to an unbearable pitch.

Justin grabbed the straps and yanked. They tore, freeing him.

He came to his senses kneeling in the snow beside the car, with the ruined seatbelt dangling beside him and his fists clenched so tight that his nails had bitten into his palms. Dazed, Justin looked around, trying to orient himself.

His snow leopard was snarling, frantic and furious. *Kill! Kill! Kill!*

"Calm down," Justin said. His voice cracked; his throat was raw. Had he been yelling? "It's all right. We're free."

His snow leopard's blind rage cooled into hatred. *The doctor. Kill the doctor.*

Justin opened his mouth to agree, then forced himself to say, "I'll *find* the doctor. Then we'll see what happens."

Kill him, insisted his snow leopard. *He hurt us.*

It was tempting. But he'd had enough of killing just because someone told him to. If there was one thing that could make the man he was now different from Subject Seven, it was making his own choices.

"We'll see," Justin said firmly.

He got back in the car, closed his eyes, and cautiously recalled touching Dr. Attanasio, keeping himself at a mental distance so he wouldn't drown in his own memories.

Where are you, doctor?

Justin felt a tug inside his mind. It wasn't the knowledge of a location, let alone an address, just a sense that his target was *that way.*

Our prey, corrected his snow leopard.

Justin began to drive *that way*, following that inner pull. He hoped it wouldn't be too far. For all he knew, he was trying to drive to China.

But it turned out that Dr. Attanasio hadn't gone far; he hadn't even left the state. The sense of *that way* ended at an apartment in San Francisco.

Justin staked out the building until he saw Dr. Attanasio leave. Then he deactivated his security system, slipped inside, and searched the place.

Based on what he found on the doctor's laptop and papers, Dr. Attanasio was no longer working for Apex, but was now busy designing extra-addictive drugs. Disgusted, Justin placed several bugs in the apartment, then replaced everything exactly the way he'd found it. He checked to make sure he hadn't missed anything and all his bugs were perfectly concealed before he stepped into a shadowy corner to wait for the doctor to return.

We lie in wait, hissed his inner snow leopard, sending Justin a sense of his satisfaction. Lying in wait was the big cat's favorite thing.

Justin sank into the calm, cool mindset of the predator within. He wasn't bored or restless. He didn't think. He just waited. It felt good. Almost like being invincible…

His snow leopard stirred in alarm. He hated Justin's power of adrenaline invincibility, which had the side effect of suppressing his inner predator.

You don't need invincibility, the big cat hissed. *You just need to lie in wait.*

I can't lie in wait all the time, Justin returned. *Now hush.*

Hours later, the door opened. Dr. Attanasio stepped inside, flicking on the light as he shut the door behind him.

Justin closed the distance between them in an instant, twisting the doctor's arms behind him with one hand and putting his other hand over Dr. Attanasio's mouth.

Kill him, snarled his snow leopard. *Rip out his throat!*

Justin mentally distanced himself from the big cat's rage. He kept his voice calm and low as he addressed the doctor. "Scream, and I'll kill you. When I take my hand away, you can talk, but do it quietly. Nod if you understand."

With his keen predator's senses, Justin could smell the acrid scent of the doctor's cold sweat. Trembling, Dr. Attanasio nodded.

Justin released the doctor and stepped in front of him.

"Subject Seven!" Dr. Attanasio gasped.

"Surprise," Justin remarked, deadpan.

"How did you find me?" The doctor's voice rose in terror. Justin dipped his hand, palm down, in a 'lower your voice' gesture. Dr. Attanasio continued, hushed but frantic. "I wore gloves every time I had to lay hands on you. And I never let you touch me. So someone must have sold me out! Who?"

Justin kept his face still, making sure he didn't reveal anything with so much as a blink. "Who do you think?"

"One of the doctors? They were always jealous of me, because *my* experiments got results." Studying Justin's face, Dr. Attanasio said, "Or was it one of the project managers? It was, right? Which one?"

Justin concealed his satisfaction. So Dr. Attanasio *was* in touch with some other survivors from Apex. In case he hadn't mentioned everyone he knew about, Justin let one of his eyebrows raise slightly and made a small, involuntary-seeming head-shake.

Yesss, hissed his snow leopard, with immense satisfaction. *We play with our prey.*

"It wasn't any of them?" Dr. Attanasio looked baffled, then even more scared. "Who was it, then? Who? There's no one else who knows where I—" He broke off, obviously realizing that he'd revealed too much.

"That's what you think," Justin said. With any luck, Dr. Attanasio would get on the phone to his evil co-workers and demand that they tell him who else was out there.

Before the doctor had a chance to collect himself, Justin slowly reached out with his bare hand, letting Dr. Attanasio see it coming.

The doctor flinched. "Don't hurt me!"

Justin had been trying to keep as cool on the inside as he looked on the outside, but something snapped inside him at those words. "Why the hell shouldn't I? You hurt me until I hoped I'd die just to make it stop!"

Dr. Attanasio flinched again, but there was no remorse in his expression, only fear. Defensively, he said, "It was necessary. We made huge scientific breakthroughs. Anyway, look what you got out of it. The Ultimate Predator process gave you powers beyond anything normal humans or even shifters can dream of. Sure, the process wasn't pleasant, but we didn't do you any harm."

"No harm?" A bitter rage burned through Justin, hot and painful as the chemical the doctor had injected into his veins while he lay strapped to the lab table. *"No harm?* You—"

He forced himself to stop. He didn't want to give the doctor the satisfaction of knowing he'd gotten to him. More importantly, he didn't want to show weakness in front of the man who would undoubtedly be reporting back to his other enemies the instant he left the room. But inside his mind, the rest of his thought echoed:

You ruined my life. You broke me.

His snow leopard hissed reprovingly. *None of that is true.*

Rather than get into a pointless argument with his snow leopard, Justin forced his attention out of his head and to the enemy in front of him. He seized his prey by the throat. The doctor let out a shrill squeal of terror.

"I'm touching you now," Justin said. "And you know what that means."

Dr. Attanasio just stared at him, his eyes bulging with panic.

"Say it," Justin said. "Say it so I know you understand."

"I can't speak when you're strangling…" Dr. Attanasio's voice trailed off as he realized that Justin had only wrapped his fingers around his throat, and wasn't exerting any pressure. "Uh, it's your Ultimate Predator power. I mean, it's one of them. You can track me now. Anywhere in the world, as far as we know. You don't need to know where I am. You just follow my—"

Scent, hissed his snow leopard. With immense satisfaction, he added, *You can run, but you can't hide.*

"—imprint," the doctor concluded.

"That's right." Justin increased the pressure, just slightly. "Are you really making designer drugs, or is that a front for Apex?"

"Apex is gone!" Dr. Attanasio choked out. "You and Subject Eight destroyed it yourselves. It's just the drugs, I swear!"

Justin considered seeing if he could squeeze more information out of him, then decided to stick with his first plan. Threatening him more might just scare him into saying whatever he imagined Justin wanted to hear.

"It better be," Justin said. "If I ever find out that you're involved in kidnapping or experimenting on unwilling subjects or anything else like what you did at Apex, I'll track you down, just like I tracked down some of your other colleagues. And I'll do to you exactly what I did to them."

Dr. Attanasio's eyes bulged even more, reminding Justin of a bullfrog. "What? Who else did you track down? Did you kill them?"

Justin stared into the doctor's pop-eyes, silent and expressionless. He knew the effect his gaze had on people, even when he didn't have them by the throat. Sure enough, the doctor gulped and looked away, blood draining out of his face until it went an unpleasant pasty color.

Without a word, Justin turned his back and walked out of the apartment, letting the door slowly close behind him.

Where are you going? His snow leopard's hiss rose in frustration. *Kill him, kill him!*

An overwhelming weariness washed over Justin. He was so tired of arguing with his snow leopard. If the big cat wasn't demanding someone's death, he was all the way on the other extreme, insisting that too-good-to-be-true things like mates and packs and happiness were just around the corner.

They are not too good to be true, hissed his snow leopard. *Remember how you insisted that your packmate had abandoned you, and I kept telling you he'd come back for you? Who was right about that?*

You were, Justin admitted. But he didn't want to talk about Shane. He could hardly bear to think about his old best friend. Trustworthy Shane, whom Justin hadn't trusted. Loyal Shane, whom Justin had betrayed.

To get his snow leopard off the topic, Justin said, *Stop calling him my packmate. Leopards don't have packs.*

Shifters do, his snow leopard retorted. *Go back inside, kill our prey, and then go to your pack. They will help us hunt down the rest of our enemies. We have spent far too long hunting alone.*

For what felt like the millionth time, Justin explained, *We need to leave him alone for now, so he thinks it's safe to talk to his colleagues. We're not doing anything to any of them until we find out where the Apex base is*. Then *we—*

Rip out their throats, hissed his snow leopard.

Justin shrugged. Maybe he'd kill them, or maybe he'd phone in an anonymous tip to the FBI and put them behind bars. Based on his own experience, suffering in captivity was a fate worse than death, so he leaned toward throwing them in jail. But his leopard seemed incapable of understanding that argument.

He ran along the corridor, his soft-soled shoes making barely more sound than a cat's paws, and opened the door to the emergency staircase. It had a sign warning that an alarm would go off if it was opened, but he had deactivated the alarm before he'd entered the doctor's apartment.

When he reached the roof, he lay down so no one could see his silhouette. Justin doubted that anyone was looking for him, other than possibly Dr. Attanasio, but stealth had become a habit, and he didn't want to get killed before he'd made sure that Apex was gone for good.

Flat on his belly atop the sun-warmed concrete, he took out his earbuds, stuck them in his ears, and listened to the sounds inside the doctor's apartment. He heard rustling, footsteps, and then the doctor saying, "Hello?"

Justin couldn't hear the response; Dr. Attanasio must be talking on his cell phone, which Justin hadn't been able to bug. But he could hear every word the doctor said, loud and clear.

"Subject Seven is alive! He broke into my apartment…" The doctor detailed what had happened, then said, "No, I'm only in touch with you. Do you know anything about anyone else? They have to be warned… if it's not too late already."

There was a brief pause in which Justin wondered who he was talking to. It had to be either a doctor or a project manager, but that could be a lot of people.

Dr. Attanasio exclaimed, "Mr. Bianchi is out of his mind if he thinks he's safe in London! You want to bet that an ocean is enough to stop Subject Seven? I wouldn't! Tell Mr. Bianchi to hire every bodyguard he can lay his hands on."

Another pause. "No, I don't know if he ever touched any of us. I thought he hadn't touched me… until now. So either we have a rat or he got our imprints on the sly or his power doesn't work the way he said it did and all he ever needed to do was fucking *smell* us!"

I wish *all we needed to do was scent our prey,* hissed his snow leopard.

I wish I'd had the sense to pretend my power worked differently, Justin replied. *I should've told them I needed to lay my entire palm on someone's bare skin for five minutes. Then they'd have been less careful around me, and I could've gotten all their imprints.*

A wave of self-reproach swept over him, so intense that he could taste the bitterness, like he'd chewed on an aspirin. It was such a simple idea, but it hadn't occurred to him until it was too late. He hadn't been smart or sneaky or quick enough to touch them all.

He hadn't saved his buddies.

He'd betrayed Shane. He'd betrayed himself. He'd—

Pay attention, hissed his snow leopard. *Our prey is speaking again.*

Justin dragged his attention back to the doctor, who was saying, "What's he doing there, anyway?"

Another pause. The doctor gave a bitter chuckle. "Of course. Mr. Bianchi's getting fabulously wealthy dealing weapons, and I'm stuck making goddamn designer drugs. And I can't ever go back to Apex, or Subject Seven will come back and… No, I told you, he didn't say who he'd killed, let alone how he'd done it. But I saw his eyes. That's not a man. That's a predator. I'm staying right where I am. Anything else would be suicide."

Dr. Attanasio said no more. The conversation was clearly over.

Justin rolled over and looked up at the darkening sky. At long last, he had a lead on one of the higher-up men at Apex, one he'd never been able to touch. London was a big city, but Justin felt confident that given enough time, he could find Mr. Bianchi there. And Mr. Bianchi might know where the base was, or know who did. If not, Justin could return to San Francisco and stalk Dr. Attanasio until he figured out who the doctor had been talking to.

No matter what, this was a big break. He should be glad. But he felt nothing but the pain that had been tearing him apart ever since he'd escaped Apex, a searing agony of rage and guilt, shame and loss, memories of a past he couldn't stand to recall and fear for a future stretching out ahead of him like a million miles of bad road. It was in his ears like a shriek of metal on metal, in his chest like a knife in the heart, in his bones with an ache like he hadn't slept in weeks. It was with him every moment of every day.

Except when he was invincible.

Don't, hissed his snow leopard.

Justin barely heard him. Dr. Attanasio's words were echoing inside his mind, loud enough to drown out everything else:

That's not a man. That's a predator.

All those cruel days and lonely nights at Apex, he'd dreamed and dreamed about escape. Then he'd gotten out, and realized that there was no escape. He could get away from Apex, but he couldn't get away from himself. Everything he'd done—everything that had been done to him—everything he'd become—was irrevocable. He couldn't change it. The best he could do was make himself not care.

Luckily, there was a way to do that.

Don't! His snow leopard gave a low growl that probably would have made Dr. Attanasio faint with terror. *You are doing it too much. It will kill you.*

Justin tried to squelch his automatic response, but his snow leopard caught it anyway:

Who cares?

The big cat's anger, fear, and frustration surged through Justin as he snarled in desperation, *I care!* I *want to live!*

At that, Justin felt guilty. He fished for some reply that his snow leopard would find reassuring and that would be honest. His inner predator was a part of him, after all; he couldn't lie to himself.

He settled on, *I have no intention of dying just yet.*

It was true, as far as it went: he had no intention of dying until he'd destroyed Apex and could be sure they'd never harm anyone again. After that, he didn't care what happened to him. But since he was wildly unlikely to survive going up against an entire black ops agency all by himself, he didn't have to worry about the "after that."

He closed his eyes and pictured himself standing alone on a vast, featureless plain of blinding white. An ice field. He imagined the ice creeping up over his feet and up his legs, at first so cold that it burned, and then numbing. When the ice reached his heart, the burning flared into agony. Justin gritted his teeth, knowing that the pain would be brief. A moment later his heart went numb, and a blessed calm washed over him.

He opened his eyes. He was alone on the roof, as alone as he'd been on his imaginary ice field. Justin couldn't feel his snow leopard. He couldn't feel anything at all. No guilt, no anger, no shame, just a cool readiness to do whatever was needed.

No pain.

He could recall anything that had happened to him at Apex, and feel nothing. If someone shot him, he'd feel nothing. He wouldn't get hungry or tired. He didn't need to eat or sleep. He was unstoppable.

Invincible.

I wish I could be like this all the time, Justin thought as he headed back for the stairs. *It feels so much better.*

The only reason he didn't was that if he stayed invincible too long, he'd die.

You have to eat and sleep to live, and when he was invincible, he not only didn't need to, he *couldn't.* And while a man could go a month or so without food, Apex experiments had shown that if he went for more than a week without sleep, his body started dangerously breaking down.

Don't worry, he said silently, though he knew his snow leopard couldn't hear or speak. *I won't keep it up long enough to do any damage. Just a few hours. Eight, max.*

Justin imagined he could hear the big cat's angry hiss:

Liar.

Made in the USA
Lexington, KY
20 August 2019